D0436488

Z

On

Location

★ American Girl®

Z
On
Location

By J. J. Howard

Scholastic Inc.

Published by Scholastic Inc., *Publishers since 1920*. SCHOLASTIC and associated logos are trademarks and/or registered trademarks of Scholastic Inc. The publisher does not have any control over and does not assume any responsibility for author or third-party websites or their content.

Book design by Suzanne LaGasa

Author photo by April Mersinger Photography

Cover photos: girl: Michael Frost for Scholastic

Gabriela excerpt by Teresa Harris

ISBN 978-1-338-13706-4

10 9 8 7 6 5 4 3 2 1   17 18 19 20 21
Printed in the U.S.A. 58 • First printing 2017

For my mom

▶ **Contents**

Chapter 1

Summer Adventure

I leaned way back in my chair and nearly fell onto the floor laughing. My friend Lauren was doing a ridiculous dance to the song playing in the Beanery and lip-synching into her tea like it was a microphone. "I almost shot bubble tea out of my nose!" I said, wiping up a bit that had spilled on the floor.

Lauren's goofing around only added to my great mood. Today was the day I'd been waiting for—and counting down to—for what felt like forever: the first day of summer vacation.

And first on our summer vacay bucket list was hitting the Beanery, our favorite hangout in town, which lucky for us was owned by our friend Mariela's parents. Lauren had to get in her last bubble tea before going to

San Diego for soccer camp. I was going to miss her so much.

"When are you going hiking with your parents? Do we have time to work on an idea for another American Girl stop-motion movie?" Lauren asked.

"We could, but I'm not sure how much we can get done. You're leaving tomorrow and won't be back for a month! I wish you were going to be here for some more summer adventures . . ."

"I know." Lauren nodded. "I'm missing out on so much with you guys, but I thought having an idea for a movie would help keep me going. Like it would give me something to look forward to when I got home."

Lauren was right. Mari and I had made a list of fun things to do over summer break here in Seattle, like trying kayaking in Moss Bay, picnicking at an out-door movie at Magnuson Park, and I wanted to get some funny "footage" at the Giant Shoe Museum. (Mari told me that joke sounded like one of my dad's.) I knew Lauren was going to have an awesome time at camp, but I was sad she was going to miss out on our adventures, too.

Just then, an alert dinged on my phone. It was a new video post by my idol, superstar vlogger Winter Costello.

She constantly knew about the most interesting stuff, like where to find the best music videos or hottest new books or cool magazine articles. Plus, her videos were amazing. She was always doing something unusual and fun. Sometimes, if I needed a surge of inspiration, I'd rewatch one of her vlogs on filming or video editing, and it always worked.

I read the title of the video in disbelief. "Lauren, you've got to see this."

Lauren stood up behind me and I read out loud: "Winter Costello: #summeradventure challenge." I turned to look at Lauren. Her eyes were wide with the same surprise I was feeling.

"Oh. My. Gosh." I looked around. "I think Winter Costello can hear me! I was *just* talking about . . ."

"Summer adventures!" Lauren continued. "Let's hear what she has to say."

I opened the video in full screen, turned the volume up, and pushed PLAY. Winter's hair was a different color in every vlog she posted, and this time, it was a light silvery blue with rad baby bangs.

"Hi, gang, Winter Costello here. Happy summer! I hope you guys have lots of fun plans, because I'd like to share a new idea with all of you."

I made a happy little squeak, but Lauren held her finger to her lips in a *shh* sign.

"When I was a kid, I always tried to cram as many new experiences as possible into summer vacation. So this year, I'm challenging myself to recapture some of that same spirit. Whether you're still a student, or if you're mostly grown-up like me, I challenge you to get outside your comfort zone this summer. Go somewhere you've never been, even if it's in your own neighborhood. Learn a new skill. Tell me about the new things you try using the hashtag #summeradventure. I'll be posting my first one soon—and I can't wait to see what all of you are up to. And the best part, because I love you guys so much, at the end of the summer, the person with the most adventury adventure will be featured right here on my vlog! Happy summer, and good luck!"

I turned around to face Lauren. "It's a sign! You know I want to be exactly like Winter Costello when I grow up." I paused. "Well, a combination of my mom and Winter. This seals it. I *have* to have the biggest summer adventures now."

Lauren sipped her tea and scrunched her eyebrows together. "I wish I could stay with you guys. I mean, I'm psyched about soccer camp, too, but . . ."

"Don't worry—we still have July and most of August! In the meantime, you're already going to have a summer adventure, starting tomorrow at soccer camp."

"That's true." Lauren grinned in anticipation. "The camp has outings planned for us on the weekends and everything, so it will be fun to explore a new city. And I heard a rumor that some of the US women's soccer team are coming for a day! You're right, Z. It *is* my summer adventure."

I had to admit that made me a little jealous. Summer excursions in a new place with famous athletes definitely sounded like awesome hashtag material.

My phone dinged. "Time for the hike. I have to go meet my parents." It wasn't exactly an adventure, but it was still going to be fun to get out of Seattle and into the Cascade mountains.

I walked Lauren outside, and we unlocked our bikes and hugged good-bye. Being apart was the one bad thing about summer vacation.

I waved until she was completely out of view and then pedaled home.

My mom was all decked out in her hiking gear when I got back. She looked so excited, I couldn't help but smile.

"It's a gorgeous day! Why don't you go upstairs and get your backpack—oh, and bring your video camera. We'll be able to see for miles."

It might not win me that spot on Winter's vlog, but it was a start.

#summeradventure here I come!

The views of Mount Rainier from our hike in the national park were amazing. I adjusted my camera and stopped to record the view. My parents and I came here pretty often, but it seemed different every time.

"Come on, slow poke," my dad called from farther up the path. My dalmatian, Popcorn, nudged my side, as though herding me to catch up to my parents.

"Coming!" I yelled back. I continued to record as I jogged to catch up. Popcorn gave a happy bark at our little burst of speed.

"Did you get some good footage?" Mom asked me.

"Yeah, but just the view of the mountain—you know, the usual. I'm on the lookout for something *amazing*," I told her

"Don't forget that the everyday can be pretty

amazing, too, Z," Mom told me, using her best professor voice. I knew she was probably right—after all, she wasn't just a professor, she was also an incredible documentary filmmaker. But I also knew that another #amazingview shot of Seattle wasn't going to qualify as a #summeradventure for Winter's challenge.

I pulled my phone out to see if anyone had posted a #summeradventure yet, but I stopped scrolling when a post about this summer's VidCon caught my eye.

It was an updated list of people appearing at the conference in Anaheim in ten days. I'd met my friends Becka and Gigi there last year, and this year Mariela and I were planning to meet up with them again.

I scanned the list, looking for familiar names, and then I spotted one that stood out from the rest: Winter Costello. She was going to be at VidCon!

Maybe my #summeradventure could be *meeting* Winter Costello! But surely she'd be meeting other fans there, too. I'd just have to figure out a way to make my meeting with her the best.

Dad appeared in front of me, frowning. "Are you going to continue the hike with us? Or are you planning to live here, just you and your phone?" Dad glanced around. "I mean, it's nice here, but we would miss you."

I rolled my eyes. Dad seriously couldn't resist an opening for a terrible joke. "No, sorry," I answered, "I just . . ."

Dad interrupted, "I know, I know. Technology. Come on, pumpkin."

I was energized by the idea of meeting Winter, and I went into jog mode to keep up with Dad and his much-longer legs. Popcorn ran around me in circles, happy to be moving fast again. She wasn't the sitting-still type of dog, that was for sure.

We caught up to Mom and fell into step with her.

"I'm starting to worry that she's actually going to disappear into that phone," he teased.

"Mom's the one who's been studying all the newest video technology," I told him. "I'm sure if they invent a way to do that, she'll be the first to know! She'd know how to get me out, too . . ." I mused.

"Speaking of my research . . ." Mom said. She shrugged out of her backpack. We'd reached the point in the trail where we'd rest and have our picnic before hiking back out of the park. Mom sat down right next to me and said, "I got a filmmaking grant based on the latest work I've been doing with emerging tech."

Mom's interested in how developing video tech helps us to communicate better, like doctors being able to see patients in hospitals all over the world in real time. In fact, she's working on a documentary about people in different fields who are using technology to communicate better, and share their experiences. It's pretty cool stuff.

"I'm going to be going on the road for about ten days this summer to film my documentary in Tacoma, San Francisco, and Anaheim," she continued, her eyes sparkling with excitement. "And I'd like for you to come with me."

"For real?" Me? On an actual film shoot?

Mom nodded. "For real. You'll be an apprentice—learning by doing." I grabbed my phone to text Lauren. She would be so excited for me! And then I'd have to text Mari and tell her we'd have to postpone all the stuff we were going to do together until after I got back. But before I could open my screen, Mom put her hand on my arm.

"It's going to be a tight schedule, so I'll need you to be really focused. You can't be on your phone all the time, okay?"

I pocketed my phone and gave her a hug. "This sounds amazing, Mom! I can't wait. When do we leave?" Popcorn, excited by the commotion, jumped up on us, making us laugh. She always assumed that all hugs were for her, too.

"I thought you might like the idea. We leave in three days."

"Wait, what about VidCon?" I didn't want to miss my chance to meet Winter Costello—or hang out with Becka and Gigi.

Mom's smile grew wider. "That's the best part. Our trip includes VidCon. I have a number of interviews set up there already, and I'm working on a few more. I have one person in particular I think you'll be interested in meeting."

I stood up, suddenly too excited to sit. "Winter Costello?" I asked, hardly believing that my dream of meeting my idol might actually come true.

"Yes. I know how much you love her! And depending on how the first shoots go, I thought you might do more than meet her. You might be ready to do your own interview with her by then."

"Are you serious? YES. I'm totally in!"

"That's what I was hoping for," Mom said. "And then after VidCon, I thought you and I could continue our road trip for a few weeks. Purely mother-daughter time."

"Sounds great, Mom!"

"Then it's a plan! Help me lay out this blanket, okay?" She stood up and we spread out the blanket together. Dad started setting up our picnic lunch. I sat back on the blanket, in total shock, staring into space as the view of Seattle below us was replaced by my vision of all the new subscribers my channel could get if I posted my *own* interview with Winter Costello.

Mom must have noticed I was daydreaming. "One step at a time, Z," she said, interrupting my thoughts. "Remember, the interview isn't a given. You'll need to prove yourself on the shoot first. I'm planning to give you a lot of responsibility—starting with being in charge of the sound recording. Do you think you can stay focused to learn the skills you need?"

I felt a little stab of disappointment. Not only because the interview wasn't a sure thing. But it also stung a little to hear Mom say that she wasn't sure I had the skills I'd need to do this interview yet. I felt like I'd already come a long way as a filmmaker. I'd even placed second in the CloudSong Film Festival with my documentary short a few months ago.

I took a deep breath, then exhaled. This was a really important film for Mom, I knew that. If I wanted to be her assistant and have the chance to do the interview with Winter, I'd have to show her I was serious, too. "I can stay focused," I told her. "I'm really excited about this trip, Mom." I couldn't wait to text my friends the awesome news! I knew they were going to be almost as excited as I was.

Mom smiled and handed me a sandwich. "Good. Me, too!"

"Cheers!" I held my sandwich up to hers.

"I'll eat to that!" Dad said, tapping my ham and cheese with the edge of his tuna salad.

While I chewed my sandwich, I imagined all the chances I'd have to win the spot on Winter's vlog, including doing the interview with Winter. I thought about what I would ask her. *Who inspires you? What is the most important thing you've learned from your fans?*

"Z!" Dad snapped his fingers in front of my nose. "Where did you go?"

I shook the daydreams out of my head. "I was just thinking about the trip."

"I told you she'd be excited," Dad said knowingly to Mom. "But for now, kiddo, the chips are in your bag. Hook me up!"

I laughed as I threw him the bag. My brain was bursting with ideas about how to win Winter's #summeradventure challenge and get a spot on her vlog. This was definitely going to be the best summer yet.

Chapter 2

Z . . . Out!

I pushed PLAY on the vlog post I'd just recorded, making sure I was satisfied with it one more time.

"Hey, Z's Crew! Major announcement time. Yours truly is getting ready to head out on an amazing summer adventure. My mom is taking a road trip to shoot her new documentary film, with me as her assistant! I'm going to be in charge of sound recording, and probably a lot of other jobs, too. I'm so excited to be on a real film shoot. I hope you'll all follow along with me, and post your own adventures using the hashtag #summer-adventure. If you haven't seen Winter Costello's new post about that, you *have* to check it out! Okay, time to leave for my road trip. Z's Crew—OUT!"

Perfect! I sent the video to Mom and Dad for final approval and jumped up. I'd stacked my bags by my bedroom door last night, and I had gotten up extra early to take Popcorn for a nice long walk. I'd miss her so much, but I knew she would go crazy inside the small RV Mom had rented for our trip. There wasn't enough space in there for a dog with her energy.

"Come on, Popcorn—let's go get Mom and Dad up." I bounded into their room. "Hey, sleepyheads! Time to get cracking! You have to be *awake* to start a road trip!"

Mom opened one eye and then closed it. "A good production assistant would never wake up the director without coffee." She smiled so I knew she wasn't really mad. But I could also tell that coffee would be a very good idea.

"On it!" I told her, and sped downstairs to brew a pot. Neither of my parents seemed able to function in the morning without coffee.

The coffeepot soon stopped making its gurgling sounds, and I carefully carried two steaming mugs upstairs.

"You're a lifesaver, Z," Dad told me as I handed him one. He was already shaving. Mom was propped up in bed, at least, and she smiled gratefully when I handed her a mug.

"Almost there," she said.

"You're a blur," I told her, repeating the family joke about how fast Mom moved in the morning. (Not. Fast. At. All.)

I headed back down to pour myself a bowl of cereal and brought it to the backyard to have breakfast in my favorite spot. Popcorn followed, as always, and lay down beside me in the grass.

We live on top of Queen Anne Hill, and my seat gave me a view of Puget Sound, the Space Needle—and today, since it was clear, I could even see Mount Rainier in the distance. I was really going to miss the Seattle summer—my favorite city at my favorite time of year.

I was happy to get to spend the summer with my mom learning new video techniques, but I was thinking about everything I'd miss this summer with my friends. They'd be doing fun things without me, like going to the Japanese Garden or Olympic Sculpture Park. They'd probably post pics from the top of the Great Wheel and the Space Needle.

Mom walked out into the yard, holding what I knew was her second cup of coffee. "Hey, Z. You getting excited to leave?"

I forced a smile and nodded. "Of course!"

I could tell from the look Mom gave me that she wasn't convinced. "I guess I'm just feeling a little FOMO."

"Translation, please," Mom said.

I laughed. "Fear of Missing Out . . . on everything that's going to happen this summer here at home."

"Z, you know all those books and movies with daring heroes that you love so much?" I wasn't sure where Mom was going with this, but I nodded and put on my paying-attention face. "A lot of those heroes have to leave home to find their adventure, right?"

Mom uses movies to explain everything. And I knew she was right about how heroes had to leave home. Just like Rey from *Star Wars* or Mulan, I was going on a journey. Granted, I didn't need to save the galaxy or stop the invading Huns, but this adventure was just as important to me. It was exciting that my mom trusted me so much, and I was going to learn everything I could so I wouldn't let her down. Plus, I was determined to get that spot on Winter's vlog.

"I *am* ready to have an adventure," I told her as I patted Popcorn's furry head.

Mom looked at her watch. "We leave in half an hour. So be sure you've got your gear together."

"I do. I just need to bring it all downstairs. Come on, Popcorn." I raced to my room to scoop up my bags, then hurtled back downstairs. I saw through the front window that the RV was already parked in the driveway.

Dad was sitting in the driver's seat, and he beeped the horn when he saw me in the window. Grinning, I ran outside.

"Just checking out this sweet ride," Dad told me. "After all, it's going to be carrying both my girls. Had to make sure it was roadworthy."

At that moment, it hit me how much I'd miss my dad. He could always, always make me smile.

What I was thinking must have shown on my face, because Dad jumped out of the RV seat. "Don't be sad, Z," he said as he helped me lift my bags into the RV. "You'll be so busy on the trip, the time will fly by."

"I know. I'll still miss you, though."

"Popcorn and I will miss you, too, sweetie. But you'll be home soon, with lots of adventures to report."

"Here's to adventures!" I answered. "Speaking of which . . . I'm going to explore this home on wheels."

Dad gave me a quick hug. "Sounds good. I'll go check if Mom needs help with anything."

I climbed into the RV, pulled out my camera and hit RECORD, starting by focusing on the driver's and passenger's seats of the RV. "My dad says this is a Class-A RV, or recreational vehicle," I narrated. I walked back to the middle section and shot the dining table with its booth-like seats, and the long sofa-like seat across from it. "Here's where we'll fuel up for our shoots." I walked to the back of the RV and panned across the queen-size bed. "This is where Mom will sleep," I said. "And here's the bathroom. Check out how tiny this sink is!" I kept walking back toward the front. "Here's where I'll sleep, in this fold-out bed that's built into the wall. As you can see, we've got all the comforts of home; they're just a little smaller—and mobile." I gave a thumbs-up. "Z out!"

Popcorn hopped up into the driver's seat. I put my arms around her. "You be good for Dad, okay, girl?" She licked my face.

"Let's get on the road," Mom called from the driveway. Dad shooed Popcorn out of the driver's seat, and Mom climbed up into the RV.

I stepped back and Dad shut the side door, giving me a wave and a smile. I waved back.

"Before we go, I have a little something for you," Mom said. "Check under your seat."

I reached down and, sure enough, there was a sparkly silver bag. I pulled out a black baseball cap from under the tissue paper. The word CREW was stitched in white thread.

"I love it!" I thrust the hat onto my head and reached across to hug her. "I'm so psyched to be part of your crew."

"I'm glad to hear it. And I'm happy to be able to spend this time with you this summer, too, Z." She put her hands on the wheel and asked, "Ready for our adventure?"

"Ready!" I agreed.

Mom nodded and pulled out into the street, backing up slowly.

I settled in to the passenger's seat. Soon I'd see all kinds of new sights—and be able to record them for my vlog and Winter's #summeradventure contest. Even though I would miss Dad, my friends, and the fun Seattle summertime, I *was* excited and ready to hit the road!

Chapter 3

Roxie the Robot

Our trip started with a huge bang. Literally.

Mom took the first turn out of our neighborhood a little too fast, and the snacks I'd just stowed above the dining area flew out of the cabinets.

"Hope I didn't scare you," Mom said as she pulled over.

"I'm fine." I unbuckled my seat belt and followed Mom back to survey the damage.

We started picking up boxes of crackers and cups of instant soup. "Oh goodness—I forgot!" Mom smacked her forehead. She opened up one of the drawers and pulled out a pile of bungee cords. "The rental place gave me these, and told me to be sure to tie up anything I loaded in. Give me a hand with these, will you?"

"Sure thing," I said, chuckling. It was unusual for my super-on-top-of-it mom to forget a detail like that. It was probably because she'd been so focused on preparing every aspect of the shoot. Which made me realize I should keep studying, too, instead of just day-dreaming out the window.

For the past three days, I'd been practicing with all the equipment we'd be using on our interviews. As we secured the last cabinet's handles, I said to Mom, "I'd like to go over the microphone setup one more time."

Mom gave me her proud-professor smile. "I think that's a very good idea."

I pulled out the binder Mom had given me with all the equipment information and notes on sound record-ing. The RV started to move again as I put my feet up on the passenger's seat to get comfortable. I loved being up front next to Mom. I turned to the page about the Rode NTG-3, a handheld mic. There was a diagram of it, and Mom's note read:

This microphone uses a supercardioid pickup pattern to record sound from one direction while avoiding pickup of back-ground noise.

Whew. This was complicated stuff.

My phone dinged a few moments later. Lauren had already posted pics from soccer camp. It looked like she was having so much fun. I liked all the posts, and then wondered what Mariela was up to. She'd posted some shots of practice with her band, Needles in a Haystack. I wanted to share what I was up to, too.

I looked around the RV for something to post. My options were pretty limited. I had a binder full of complicated information about sound equipment, and some cabinets full of food (now secured with bungee cords). #RVsafety? #Funwithmicrophones?

I sighed, but then reminded myself, *You're on your way to a real film shoot.* That's the first adventure.

I had an idea. "Hey, Mom, will you make a Z's Crew post with me? I want to tell everyone how excited I am to be on a real film crew."

"Sure. If you don't mind me driving and talking."

"No—it'll be more authentic that way, since this is a filmmaking road trip."

I turned on my camera and held it out in front of me. "Greetings from the road, Z's Crew. I'm here with professional filmmaker Michelle Yang—a.k.a. Mom. We're on our way to our first shoot. Mom, can you tell my followers a little bit about the documentary?"

"Of course, Z. For the past several years, I've been

pulling together ideas for a documentary about new forms of technology, and ways that tech can help us to communicate better."

"Thanks, Mom!" I said, and turned the camera back toward myself. I beamed into it. "Z's Crew, I can't tell you how excited I am about this film. I mean, connecting with all of you through tech is kind of my thing, right? And I'm lucky to get to learn from my favorite filmmaker and my personal hero, my mom. Okay, so I'd better go finish getting ready for our first shoot. For Professor Yang and Z from Highway—where are we, Mom?"

"I-5."

"Okay, from I-5 on road trip day one, this is Z's first official #summeradventure post. See you soon! Z's Crew—out."

I leaned back in my seat. "Thanks for appearing in the vlog," I told Mom.

"No problem. How's the studying going? Have you run into any questions?"

I felt a stab of guilt, realizing I hadn't gotten very far in my studying before getting sucked into my friends' photo feeds.

"No questions yet. I think I'm ready."

"Well, good. Just let me know. We have about an hour until we reach Tacoma."

I opened my binder. I knew Winter Costello was going to be at VidCon, but I couldn't recall the specifics of the person we were interviewing first. I scanned the page and remembered the awesome story of our first interview subject, Kacey Kravitz. She was an inventor who, at only eighteen years old, already had a patent for a robot that she created to help kids with learning difficulties understand how to interact with others.

I read about Kacey's background—science fair wins, graduating two years early from high school. I couldn't wait to meet her. I wondered if she'd let me post something about her new work for #summeradventure.

After I'd read up on Kacey, I went back to studying the mic information. As Mom always said: A good film-maker is always prepared!

We were meeting Kacey at her dorm on the Tacoma campus of the University of Washington. Mom steered the RV into a parking space, and then she got out her clipboard with the checklist of everything we needed for the shoot. I started to feel excited butterflies in my stomach as I put on my CREW hat, loaded myself up with gear, and followed Mom toward the building. A real film shoot—this was it! I couldn't wait to show my mom everything I knew. I was going to be the best assistant she ever had!

Kacey spilled out of the double doors with some other students as soon as we got close. "Hi! You must be Michelle! I'm Kacey."

"It's so nice to meet you," Mom said. "And this is my production assistant, Z. Also known as my daughter!"

I blushed a bit, but then quickly said, "Thanks for holding the doors. I wasn't sure how we were actually going to open them."

"Oh, here, let me take one of your bags," said Kacey.

"Thank you so much," Mom said. "Just please be very careful setting it down—that case has some camera lenses in it."

"Basically every bag and case in our house has camera equipment in it," I told Kacey. "You get used to setting everything down gently."

Mom smiled at me and rolled her eyes at my teasing. We always teased each other, but suddenly I wasn't sure whether I should be more formal when we were on a shoot like this. Kacey was close to my age, though—and so friendly—that I felt more relaxed than I'd expected to on the first shoot.

"I thought we'd do the interview right here in the common room, if that's okay," Kacey said to Mom. "There's plenty of space."

"Sounds great—and there's lots of light!" Mom said as she looked around at the many windows. "Okay, Z, let's get everything set up. I think we'll be fine with one camera for today. I'll get started on that setup. Can you open up the mic case and get going on that end?"

"Sure thing!" I ran over to the case, and *thump*! I tripped over another bag I had set on the ground.

"Cool move, huh?" I said, trying to cover up my klutziness.

"It will only take us a couple of minutes to get set up," my mom told Kacey.

Great, I thought. I couldn't even smoothly handle one of the first tasks Mom gave me.

"No rush, Michelle." Kacey came over to see what I was doing. "So you're in charge of the sound?"

"Yup," I told her. "This is actually our first shoot for the film, so I'm still learning."

Kacey picked up the mic I'd chosen to use—the one I'd read most about seemed like it would work well. "Nice microphone—is it a condenser or dynamic mic?"

My first pop quiz! "It's a condenser mic. We'll use it to pick up your voice without any background interference in the interview." Nailed it.

"Sorry to be nosy," Kacey said. "My robots are all equipped with microphones so that they can seem to interact with the kids. Studying sound equipment has become one of my new obsessions."

"Can you come on the rest of the trip with us?" I joked. "There's so much to learn!"

"I'd love to, but I'm stuck here getting this project ready for Roxie's next public appearance."

"Roxie?" I knew Kacey had created a robot, but I didn't know it had a name.

"You'll see in a minute."

I fumbled a bit setting up the condenser mic, but I eventually figured it out. Maybe I should have practiced putting this together instead of just reading over Mom's notes.

Mom called out to me to see if I was ready.

"All set," I answered, snapping the last connection in place. I think I had it right.

"Okay, guys, you can bring Roxie out!" Kacey called.

Kacey's friends appeared, each holding one arm of a bright-pink robot wearing a University of Washington ball cap.

They set it down on a low table and hit a button on its back. The robot whirred to life. Blue lights flashed from its eyes, and one pink arm raised in a wave.

Kacey patted her leg. "Meet Roxie the Robot!"

Both Mom and I clapped. "She's not what I was expecting," I said. "She seems so . . ."

"Do I seem smart?" Roxie asked, and I burst out laughing.

"Roxie is programmed to pick up on more than a thousand words and phrases and frame an appropriate response." I looked over at Mom and saw that she'd removed her camera from its tripod and was capturing Kacey introducing her robot. *Lesson one*, I thought. *Always be ready to film on the fly.*

"Say hello, Roxie."

"Hello. Would you like to shake my hand?"

I giggled and reached down to shake the metal hand.

"Sorry her hands are cold," Kacey apologized. "I'm working on a way to make them warmer, and add some degree of softness."

Mom captured some more footage of Roxie the Robot interacting with me, and then she directed Kacey to the seat she'd selected for the interview.

I stood beside Kacey but made sure my mic—and I—were out of the frame. Mom asked Kacey a few questions about Roxie. Kacey was relaxed and funny, and the interview flew by as she explained that her cousin, who was on the autism spectrum, was her inspiration to create the robot. Roxie provided a safe way for kids to practice interacting with others.

"Okay, I think we've got what we need. Thank you so much, Kacey," Mom said.

"Why did you decide to make her pink?" I asked.

"It's my cousin's favorite color. I do have plans to make ones in different colors, too, but I have to admit, I love the pink."

Roxie's pink head nodded and the blue lights of her eyes twinkled. "Roxie is happy!" The robot twirled around twice, and we all laughed. I could see how kids would really respond to her. Before we broke down the set, I pulled out my phone to snap a few pics of it for a #summeradventure post I'd put up when we got back to the RV.

We waved good-bye to Kacey and Roxie after we were all packed up. I carefully balanced the bags I was carrying while we walked so I could thumb through my photos to find the best one for my post. I couldn't wait to show my friends what a real film set looked like.

"That was a great first day," I told Mom as I hoisted the case I was carrying higher on my shoulder. I had to admit, even that short interview had been hard work. I didn't want Mom to see how tired I was.

"Yes, Kacey was a very relaxed subject. Let's get our gear packed up in the RV and then we can go get some ice cream to celebrate a successful first shoot."

"Bring it on! Z is happy!" I twirled twice, just like Roxie had done. Mom laughed at my robot impression. Once we reached the RV, Mom asked me to double-check our equipment to make sure nothing was left behind.

I ran through the list: Cameras, check. Mics, check. Adapter cables, uh-oh.

"I'll be right back, Mom!" I sprinted back toward the dorm, just as Kacey was coming out with the cables in hand.

"I saw these under the table and hoped I'd catch you!" she said.

"Thanks! I can't believe I forgot them." I was so embarrassed, but Kacey just smiled and said, "It happens. Safe travels!"

I ran back to the RV, hoping I could get the cables packed without Mom noticing, but no such luck. "Maybe next time we should bring the checklist to the set with us?" she said, putting a hand on my shoulder.

Before we headed out for ice cream, I had to post about the day. I had led some shoots for my CloudSong short film, but that was nothing compared to a real, professional shoot. I was happy I'd learned enough about sound equipment to get it right, and except for leaving cables behind, I really felt like I'd earned my CREW hat today. I went to stand in front of some of the equipment in the back of the RV and took a selfie in my gear.

Once I had a good shot, I typed the caption:

Day One: life on the road making this documentary. #filmcrew #lifeontheroad #summeradventure #robotedition

Hopefully, my followers would think this was as cool as I did. And even more, I hoped they couldn't tell how wiped out from the day I felt. I was ready for that ice cream.

Chapter 4

The Wrong Kind of Mic Drop

My phone dinged really early, and I opened it to see it was another #summeradventure post from Winter. I immediately hit PLAY. She was wearing a helmet and standing in what looked like a giant forest.

"Hey, gang! Wow, you guys have been getting your adventures on hard already! I have seen some amazing posts from you all. It's going to be a hard decision when it comes to who gets that special feature on my vlog! You guys inspired me to do even more adventurous stuff, so here I am, hundreds of feet in the air, ready for my first-ever canopy tour! I hope you don't have a fear of heights!"

I took a deep breath, half afraid for Winter, and half afraid that my posts wouldn't stack up to the rest.

Winter's camera wobbled while she strapped it into

her helmet and launched off the platform. Winter whooped and I could totally understand why. I felt like I was flying through the tops of the trees! I had to try that! When she landed, the camera wobbled again while she took the camera off.

"That was amazing! You guys, wow! What an adrenaline rush! Keep your videos coming, I'm going back up to do that again! Bye!"

Oh my gosh. How was I going to compete with that kind of adventure? I was going to have to step up my game. I was going to have to be on the lookout for awesome post material today.

I stood with my mouth open, gazing up at high ceilings set with flat screens showing footage of fast-moving cityscapes. *This* was our next interview location? It was seriously impressive. I shot a few seconds of video from my phone. Maybe I could edit that together with some other shots from the day for my post.

"Ms. Danvers," I heard Mom say, "this is my daughter, Z. She's my assistant on the shoot today. Z, this is Calista Danvers, the CEO and founder of Cortex."

I dragged my eyes from the ceiling. The tall, impressive-looking woman in the pale blue suit in front of us held out her hand and I grabbed it to shake. She had a superfirm grip that seemed about right for an important CEO of a technology company. "Follow me, ladies. We can do the interview in my office as we discussed."

I'd read up on Cortex in Mom's binder of information. Cortex sold systems that let you communicate with lots of different devices in your home, from setting or checking your security system remotely to checking on your kids. They were pioneering all kinds of sensors to be built into homes—ones that would tell you if the air filter needed to be changed, or even if the house was shifting on its foundation. It reminded me of a story about a futuristic house we'd read in language arts class. I wondered if I could work that into my post somehow.

Calista's office was just as awe-inspiring as the lobby. Her desk alone was the size of my room at home. I probably couldn't fit the whole thing into a shot from my camera. "Z, can you start getting the B camera set up? We don't have much time," Mom was saying. The sharp tone in her voice told me this wasn't the first time she'd asked me. Whoops. I needed to focus.

"On it!" I called, and knelt to unzip the camera bag I carried, setting up the tripod as quickly as I could.

Mom and Calista had walked over to her desk, and Mom was setting up the A camera in front of it, so that must be where Calista would sit to answer Mom's questions. I saw that Mom was handling everything really smoothly, but it took me a couple of tries to get the camera to sit correctly in the tripod. I felt my frustration build, knowing I'd practiced this setup a bunch of times. I guess being distracted didn't make me the best assistant.

Mom appeared beside me. "You need to move much faster, Z," she said in a low voice. "I've already got the A camera in place. I was hoping you could fit the lav mic on Calista, to get the practice, but I've already done it. We need to get this all set up more quickly."

Mom snapped the camera into place and checked the settings. "This camera is going to be our backup," she told me, speaking fast. "On some shoots we'll use the B camera to get alternate shots, but on this one we're racing against the clock. I need you to set up the shotgun mic and get in place with that so I can start the interview. Got it?"

"Got it," I said, my frustration continuing to grow. Everything had gone so smoothly with Kacey and Roxie, but today I was slowing Mom down.

I unpacked the handheld microphone, moving double time, and checked the settings. I stood behind Calista's impressive desk, just out of the shot, and gave Mom a thumbs-up that I was ready.

"Just a minute and I'll be ready, too," she called back.

My phone buzzed in my pocket and I pulled it out. Mari had texted me.

> **MARIELA:** Did you see Winter's vid!!?? Are you going to post a #summeradventure today? Can't wait to see!

My fingers itched to push PLAY and see what Winter's newest post was all about, but focusing on the interview was more important. I quickly texted back.

> **Z:** Yes to both! On set w/ Mom wish me luck!

Mari texted back right away.

MARIELA: Good luck xoxo! Also check this video out. I went to Woodland Park! Have you ever heard of a wallaroo? Adorable!

She'd sent a video, but I knew I couldn't watch it now, no matter how tempting. Mari sent a few more cute wallaroo pics and selfies though. It looked like she was having so much fun and I wondered if Calista would mind if I took a picture of her for a #summeradventure post. Maybe I should be stealthy and just do a selfie . . .

"Z, are you ready to record?"

Whoops. Mom had totally seen me with my phone out.

"Ready," I answered guiltily, putting my hand with the phone in it slowly behind my back and sliding it into my pocket.

"Audio and video are rolling," Mom announced.

She stepped away from the A camera a little to start the interview.

"Ms. Danvers, can you tell me a bit about the kinds of new technology your company is creating?"

Already this interview felt very different from our first. I remembered that Mom had said that Kacey was a "very relaxed subject." Calista Danvers seemed really busy, and we didn't have as much time as we did with Kacey. The whole thing felt like a bigger challenge.

I made myself focus on what Calista was saying. "Here at Cortex, we're most interested in the area of sensors. Sensors aren't machines—they don't make anything. What they do is collect data. Our job, then, is finding a way to make that data meaningful—to people and devices. For example, we are exploring the ways that sensors can help us to build the perfect home. One that . . ."

My concentration was broken again when my phone buzzed in my pocket. I should have turned it off instead of leaving it on vibrate. I hoped the mic wasn't sensitive enough to pick up that sound. But the look on Mom's face said it definitely was.

"Cut!" Mom said. Calista looked over at me, and I set the mic down and pulled my phone out to switch it all the way off.

"I'm so sorry, I thought I had it turned off." Calista didn't say anything, but she looked at her watch.

We started rolling again right away. I was so embarrassed, I closed my eyes for a second to refocus. Mom had made a point to tell me that she needed me to focus when I was working with her—and she'd specifically warned me *not* to get distracted by my phone.

When I opened them, I glanced at the video monitor and saw that the mic had dipped down into the frame.

Calista stopped speaking, and both she and Mom turned to look at me. I felt my face get warm. "Sorry."

"Do you need me to start again?"

"No, Calista, I'm sorry," Mom said. "We can add some B-roll over part of your answer to cover the mic. If you could just pick up with your last sentence, about the use of sensors in home foundations to communicate warnings about earthquakes?"

Calista nodded and resumed speaking. I held on to the mic as though I were a *Titanic* survivor and it was my driftwood.

Mom asked a couple more questions, and before I knew it, she was thanking Calista, and an assistant was shooing us out of the office. I carried the B camera, still on its tripod. "We'll pack up fully in the lobby," Mom said in a clipped tone as she guided me out.

"I'm so sorry," I said as soon as the assistant had left.

Mom continued breaking down the camera I'd carried. "It's okay, Z—we'll talk more about this later. For now, could you help me get all the cases closed up?"

"Okay," I answered, doing as she asked.

I didn't know exactly how the talk was going to go, but I knew one thing for sure. We were not headed out for ice cream to celebrate.

I leaned against the RV and pulled up the video Mari had sent me while we were in the interview. Mom had stepped away to make a phone call. She hadn't been very talkative while we were loading the equipment. I knew I had messed up and felt terrible about my mistakes. But Mom had said it was okay, that we could fix it. I just hoped we could.

The video was of a thing that looked like a miniature kangaroo hopping, and Mari had put one of her own songs over it so it looked like it was dancing. I was about to text Mari that it was hilarious, but then saw Mom coming and put my phone away, ready to get back on the road.

"Hold on, Z. We need to talk for a moment."

"Okay." I took a deep breath in and turned to face Mom.

She sighed. "First, I want to tell you that I'm sorry. It wasn't fair for me to expect you to be able to do everything I need an assistant to do. It's a lot of work, even for someone with experience. I thought . . . It's just that I forget your age sometimes, because you've done so much with your own filmmaking, and keeping up with your vlog. I know that takes a lot of time and energy. But you are acting as my assistant on this shoot, and I expect certain things. First, you really need to turn your phone off for the shoots. But I know I have to keep in mind that you still need some supervision on set."

"I'm really sorry I forgot, Mom," I said. "I'll definitely remember next time."

"Well, I appreciate that. Just to make things a little easier, I got us some extra help, too, for the rest of the trip. Nora, one of my students from last semester, is going to meet us at our next stop in San Francisco."

I felt my face fall. Mom didn't think I could help her at all anymore? Just because of a couple of tiny mistakes? "But—I can do it!" I protested. "We don't need more help."

"You're still an important part of the crew, Z. Having Nora here will just take some of the pressure off. She's helped me with shoots before, and she's very good. Besides, I think you'll like her."

I felt a moment of panic. "Does this mean I won't get to interview Winter?"

Mom put her arm around me. "I think that's still up in the air. Let's see how the next few shoots go, okay? Just take today as a lesson, and remember that when we're shooting, that's all we're doing."

"Okay." I knew there was nothing more to say. I slid the CREW hat from my head, feeling defeated. "Hey, do you mind if I go into the back and get started on a new vlog post?"

"Sure, honey. I'll call you when it's time to stop for a bite to eat."

I climbed up in to the RV and walked back to the kitchen area. The binder with all my training information was still lying there open, just where I'd left it. I pushed it closed. I definitely didn't want to do more studying now.

What I needed to do was connect with my friends. First, I caught up on all my friends' feeds. Lauren had posted photos from Color Wars Day at soccer camp. She looked really happy, dressed in blue from head to toe and grinning from ear to ear.

Becka had played in a tournament with her wheelchair basketball team, and they'd won. She'd posted some triumphant shots of her high-fiving her teammate, and one of the scoreboard.

Gigi was home in London, and it looked like she'd spent the day shopping with her friends. But even her regular shopping trip looked so much cooler to my eyes because: *London!*

Finally, with Mari's trip to Woodland Park, it seemed like all of my friends were having exciting and fun starts to their summer. I genuinely did "like" all of their photos, but I also felt the slightest pangs of jealousy. This trip was a lot harder and definitely less exciting and fun than I had thought it would be.

Becka texted me and Gigi just as I was scrolling through everyone's feeds.

> **BECKA:** Zzzzzzzzz!!! How's the filmmaking going??
>
> **GIGI:** Hello Z! Yes, tell us all about your glamorous summer. So jealous!

I'd just been sitting here feeling jealous of *their* summers. And wanting so badly to share with my friends about how everything seemed to be going wrong. But for some reason, hearing Gigi call my summer "glamorous" made me want them to keep seeing it that way.

z: It's amazing being on a REAL film set.
Learning so much!

Well, at least that part was true. I'd definitely learned what not to do—by messing up—in the past two days.

BECKA: Post more pics! I've been stalking your feed and haven't seen ANYTHING. You're just too busy filming, I guess. ;)

GIGI: Yes, pics! I can't believe we'll all be together at VidCon soon! And you're going to interview WINTER COSTELLO!!

Shoot. I'd told everyone about the interview after Mom told me, and I had felt totally confident that I would actually be doing the interview then.

I wasn't so sure anymore.

BECKA: I know, I can't BELIEVE it! I am so excited. HEY, Z, do you think we could sit in on the interview? Please say yes! She's so amazing . . .

GIGI: Pleeaaasssee? We will be quiet as mice so you won't even know we're there. ☺

Wishing it to be true, I typed in my response and hit SEND.

> **z**: I'll try really hard to get you guys into the interview. Promise! Can't wait to see you @VidCon!

Fake it until you make it, right? If I wanted to interview Winter Costello, I had to act like it was going to happen.

Chapter 5

Don't Ask Me Anything

"Going my way?" Nora asked, grinning as she stuck her head in the window of the RV. We'd been waiting for her at the airport for what seemed like forever, but Mom didn't seem to mind.

"Oh, Nora—thank you so much for coming on such short notice! You're a lifesaver!" Mom turned to me. "Z, this is Nora, my student—and superhero," she added with a wink at Nora. "Nora, this is my daughter, Z, an aspiring filmmaker."

"Nice to finally meet you, Z! Your mom talks about you all the time. She's really proud of those little videos you make."

Nora reached out to shake my hand. I took her hand and shook automatically. I didn't love her choice of words: *those little videos you make.* But she probably hadn't seen them to know how much work they really were.

Nora *looked* every inch the cool college film student, I had to admit. She was tall, with dark red hair, and wore an outfit that I knew would have earned Mariela's fashion guru seal of approval: black leggings with a little diamond pattern woven through them, an oversize white T-shirt with a jumble of tiny gold necklaces, and a long light blue cardigan.

"Make yourself comfortable," Mom said, and gestured to the passenger seat. "It's less than a half hour drive to the Exploratorium." And just like that, I was stuck in the back of the RV with the equipment—probably for the rest of the trip.

I wandered to the back and settled in for the drive. When we stopped, I'd have to move my stuff to my new space in the RV—I'd sleep in the big bed with Mom, and Nora would take the fold-out. I checked my phone, hoping for something interesting, but for once I didn't have any new texts or notifications. Remembering yesterday's disastrous shoot, I turned it completely off and put it in my pocket. No distractions this time! Soon we pulled into the Exploratorium, and I ventured up front where Mom and Nora were talking about the shoot.

". . . so excited that we're going to be filming in the Exploratorium's Kanbar Forum!" Nora was saying. "How amazing will it be to set up the sound in there? They have a Constellation acoustic system."

"Nora's main area of interest is sound recording, Z," Mom told me.

"Oh, you'll be handling the sound for the shoot?" I asked.

That was supposed to be my job.

"Yes, but don't worry. There's plenty of work to go around." Mom sounded reassuring. I just hoped this #summeradventure hadn't turned into a #summerbummer.

It was a lot easier carrying all our gear with another person, but that didn't make me any happier about suddenly being the third wheel. Still, maybe I could make the best of having Nora around and learn even more about sound recording on our shoots.

"So, Nora, how does a Constellation acoustic system work?" I asked as we walked inside.

"Oh," she said, not looking at me. "It's complicated. Here, can you grab this?" She handed me an extra bag.

"Sure," I said, adding her pack to my already full arms. She walked ahead to catch up with my mom. Ouch.

The inside of the Exploratorium was awesome, and I wanted to see everything—the Tinkering Studio, where you could build and experiment with all sorts of different materials, and the observatory, where you could do things like make your own solar system model and check the weather in space. But I didn't know how much time we'd have, and I wanted to be prepared, especially after the last disaster. Like Mom said, when we're shooting, that's all we're doing.

As soon as we walked in, Mom's contact greeted us, and we followed her as she fast-walked us to the place Nora had been talking about, the Kanbar Forum, which turned out to be an auditorium with a stage and rows of seats. There were three director's chairs set up onstage; that must be where Mom was going to do her interviews.

A short guy introduced himself as the "sound guru." He and Nora started speaking incomprehensible tech-speak right away. "I'm going to go help in the sound booth to adjust the levels for us, okay?" Nora asked Mom.

"Sounds good." Mom turned to me. "Z, are you ready to set up the B camera? Just like you did yesterday."

I pushed back any lingering frustration and tried to focus on proving myself today. "Sure thing."

I set up the tripod, then went to check the settings. I remembered I'd saved the note on what they should be set to in the notes app on my phone. Should I risk turning it back on?

With a sigh, I hit the POWER button. I checked the camera's settings, then stepped back and made sure to turn my phone off again. "What else can I help with?" I asked Mom.

But Nora was back from her sound mission and said, "Grab the key light, Z. It should go right here."

I looked over at Mom. Nora was giving me orders now?

Mom caught my eye and just nodded; she was busy talking to one of the interview subjects who'd just shown up.

"The angle has to be right," Nora said, adjusting the light I'd just set up in the spot she'd marked. "I'm going to run the sound. You can run the B camera. Do you know how to do that?"

I didn't trust myself to speak just then. I wanted to tell her I had already set it up and had already been doing that before she got here, but I just nodded.

All you had to do yesterday was hold the microphone, a little voice inside my head reminded me. "Sure, I can do that," I answered calmly.

The other two interview subjects showed up, and Nora showed me where I should be positioned. I stood there, feeling useless and mad at myself, watching Nora set up the lavalier mics on each of the subjects.

"Audio and video rolling," Mom said, and then she was introducing the three Exploratorium people. The first guy, Tom, said, "I'm a curator in the East Gallery, where we have exhibits focused on living systems."

"Can you tell us about some of your exhibits and how you use technology to communicate to visitors what you are showing?" Mom asked.

"Sure. One favorite is the special lenses we've developed for the plankton exhibit. The lens is a table, so visitors of all ages and heights can see the magnified images of microscopic life . . ."

I got distracted by Nora for a second as she adjusted her mic. Plankton were not the most interesting things in the universe, anyway. A few minutes later, I heard Nora call in a low voice, "Z." I focused in on her face. She nodded toward the second interview subject and motioned for me to move the B camera. Carefully, I moved the camera and the tripod.

"I'm Sally Stevens," the woman was saying. "I work in our education department. We partner with the community to plan events for local school students, as well as online learning opportunities."

"What forms of new technology are helping you to educate more people right now, would you say?" Mom asked.

While Mom fired her questions, I looked around, desperate for something to do. Something important. Something that would prove to Mom that I was able to handle more than the B camera setup.

Sally had a very intent look on her face while she spoke. Her dark eyebrows knitted together and her eyes were the most intense shade of green. A close-up would be so cool.

Not wanting to disturb the B camera, I ran over to one of our cases and pulled out another camera. I crept in for the close-up. *Crash!* I tripped over a wire on the ground and landed flat on my face. Slowly, I raised my head only to be horrified again. Shards of glass littered the ground. I had broken the lens!

Mom raced over to see if I was okay. As soon as she saw I was, her face turned beet red. "I'm so sorry for the interruption, Sally," Mom apologized. She ran back to continue the interview.

"So what new forms of technology are the most useful here at the Exploratorium?" Mom asked.

Sally blinked. It was basically the same question Mom had just asked.

My fault. My mess-up had thrown Mom off.

Nora cleared her throat and stepped out from behind her sound equipment. "Sorry, Sally. We need to get that last answer again—there was a problem with the sound. If you wouldn't mind repeating what you said about the Tinkering Studio?"

Sally's expression cleared. "Oh, no—of course not." She began repeating the same answer she'd just given. The one that perfect Nora had almost definitely managed to record perfectly.

I saw Mom give Nora a grateful smile. Me, she didn't look at again. I knew she was disappointed in me again.

And knowing that was worse right now than *hearing* how angry she was at my mess-up.

I stood next to the B camera in silence without touching—or saying—anything for the rest of the interview. I tugged my CREW cap lower, wishing I could disappear into the floor. So much for showing Mom how helpful I could be. Instead, I was showing her how *un*helpful I could be. And if I couldn't prove to Mom that I was a good and responsible assistant, I'd never get the chance to interview Winter. I was trying, but I kept messing up. Was I going to be able to do *anything* right on this trip?

Chapter 6

Be in the Now

I trudged behind Nora on our way out of the interview, carrying the fill light screen and a small case of lenses.

I'd *tried* to redeem myself by carrying one of the heaviest bags, but Nora had heroically "rescued" me, and took it right from my arms.

Aside from Nora's concern for my muscles, we finished loading up the equipment mostly in silence. Mom got behind the wheel, and Nora typed the address for the RV park into her phone. I took my seat in the back. I couldn't decide if I was glad that Mom hadn't given me a lecture yet about breaking the lens, or if I would rather have just gotten it over with.

I didn't even want to work on a vlog post, if I was honest—I just needed some cheering up.

So I pulled out my phone and watched the video

Mari sent me of the wallaroo again. And then I watched some videos I'd taken of Popcorn running around in the yard the week before. The cute videos helped take my mind off the inescapable conversation with Mom. There'd be plenty of time to worry about the next shoot and our new crew member later.

Just then, I heard someone clear their throat behind me. Mom was standing a few feet away, watching me. I realized that the RV had stopped.

"Are we at the park?" I asked Mom.

She nodded. "Nora already went out for a walk. We've been here for about five minutes already. I called you from the front, but you didn't hear me."

"Sorry. I was watching some videos."

Mom sat down next to me. "I think we should talk about a few things," she started. Man, did that sound familiar.

I jumped in with my apology right away. "I know. But can I start by saying that I'm really, really sorry for breaking the lens? I can save up my allowance to try to pay you back. I just thought I could get a great shot, one that would look so cool in your documentary. It's just that I really wanted to show you that I had what it takes as a filmmaker. I wanted to prove to you that I'm good enough to interview Winter at VidCon. I want to do that so much. It would be so cool to post that on my vlog, so my followers . . ."

"Z, hold on. I know you are trying to prove yourself and that interviewing Winter is important to you and to your vlog, but this is *my* film. I worked hard to get the grant money to make it, and this interview was important to me and my work. The bigger issue is that you need to be more present, in general, not just thinking about what might be best for you or worthy of a post or interesting to your vlog followers. We've talked about this before. You spend so much time with your face in your phone, or worrying about how many likes some future post might get . . ."

"But my phone was off today!" It seemed so unfair to get in trouble for being on my phone on a day when I'd actually turned it completely *off.* It had been hard, but I'd done it.

"You're not listening to what I'm saying, Z. This is not a conversation about whether your phone was on or off today. I'm talking about the bigger picture. I think you spend too much time living in the online world, and not enough in the actual world. The mistake you made today is a good example. When you're busy filtering reality into what it might be as a post, you're missing what's really going on, and might not read a situation correctly. Do you see what I'm saying?"

I nodded slowly. I didn't think I was that out of touch, but that *did* make sense.

"I hadn't thought about it that way before."

"Think about it now—that's all I'm asking. This trip is a great opportunity for you to have a lot of new experiences. Do you think you can try to be in the now for the rest of it?"

I nodded. "I can. I don't want to let you down, Mom."

Mom enfolded me in a hug. "You won't, sweetie, not if you try your best. Now, how about we bust out some of that instant cocoa we packed?"

"Sounds good," I told her. "I'll get the marshmallows."

As I helped make the hot cocoa, I thought about how lucky I was to have such a cool mom. I loved her so much and I knew now, more than ever, that I wanted to grow up to be just like her. Not just in the mom sense, but in the filmmaker sense, too. Now I just had to prove to Mom that I could be a valuable part of the crew—so that she would still let me do the interview with Winter. And let my friends sit in.

Tomorrow was another filming day. Another chance to be in the now.

Chapter 7

Drama Queen

"Good morning, pumpkin!" Dad said, holding up a mug of coffee for a toast on our breakfast video call. I laughed, despite still feeling a little discouraged. "How are things on the road?"

It's a lot harder than I expected. I've been messing up, but I know I can do better.

"Not the way I thought it would be," I finally said. "But I hope I'm starting to get the hang of things."

"That's my girl," Dad said. "Nothing worth doing is ever easy, you know."

"I think I've heard that a few hundred times in my life," I said. "But it's kind of different when you live it, you know?"

"I do. I'm a lot older than you. I've heard that saying *thousands* of times."

I had to laugh out loud. Trust my dad to turn a serious moment into a joke.

"Where are you going next?" Dad asked.

"Today we're filming at a camp called Drama Connect," I told him. "Mom says they're using new technology in all sorts of cool ways."

"Neat!" said Dad. "That'll be really— Uh-oh."

"Uh-oh what?"

"Someone wants her turn." Popcorn's nose filled my screen and I laughed.

"Popcorn, I miss you!"

"Heeeeeeey," Dad's voice said, and his face appeared back in the screen. "Her you miss, huh?"

"I miss you, too, Dad," I said.

"Well, it wouldn't hurt to tell me, though, would it?"

"I guess not," I said. "I miss you more than the bubble tea at the Beanery."

"Wow," Dad said, sounding surprised. "That's quite a lot."

"It really is," I agreed.

I felt a little better after talking with Dad, and I was ready to work hard and avoid any major mess-ups.

Setup at Drama Connect was going pretty smoothly. We had everything unpacked, the B camera was ready, and I was prepared to take my place behind it as soon as Mom gave the word.

Mom said she wanted to get some background footage before setting up the full interview shoot. Amara, the founder, was demonstrating the Drama Connect scene study system for us. The campers had mentors, working actors from all over the world. The instructors captured live videos of the campers' scenes, and streamed them to the mentors to view. All campers got to have a video chat with a real actor to discuss their performances.

"Can we film the actors running through this scene before we ask you some questions?" Mom asked Amara now.

"Sure thing. Okay, group two, come on up." Seven kids rushed onto the stage. They were rehearsing *A Midsummer Night's Dream*, and the camper playing Titania, the fairy queen, was very convincing. Even though she wore plain old shorts and a T-shirt, there was something about the way she carried herself that made her seem royal. Mom stepped closer to me. "So, Z, since this is a narrative scene, we're going to get some different kinds of shots," she whispered. "Will you go help Nora with the B camera? I'd like you guys to get a wide shot, and a two-shot of Titania and Bottom."

"Sure thing!" I said, then realized I'd said it a bit too loudly. I was hoping to handle B camera by myself again but didn't want to rock the boat. At. All. I quickly went down the stage steps to where Nora stood checking the settings on the camera. "We're supposed to get a wide shot and a two-shot of the main actors," I told her, remembering to whisper this time.

"Right," Nora whispered back. "Your mom gave me a shot list."

"Oh." I felt a little deflated that Nora already knew what was up. But I was determined to be positive today.

"Can you set up the fill light for the kids on the end of that line of fairies?" Nora asked me. I fought back my disappointment.

I followed Nora and carried the light. The scene was an entertaining one, especially with the little fairies. I thought it would be even more adorable once they were in their costumes, wearing tiny, sparkly wings.

"Okay, Z," Nora said when she finished filming what Mom had asked for. "Do you want to take over for a few minutes?" She stepped away from the tripod.

"Totally! Thanks, Nora." I stepped up, first lowering the tripod height by a few inches. I could stand on my tiptoes and see through the viewfinder, but Nora was a few inches taller than Mom.

I filmed the rest of the scene, right through to when all the kids took a bow. I saw Mom showing Amara where she wanted them to sit up onstage, so I knew we were about to do the interview.

"Nora," Mom said, walking to a spot between the interview subjects and Nora's tripod, "will you set up the other mic for this one? We want to reduce all the echo in the auditorium. I'm going to frame a shot locked in on Amara's head and shoulders with the A camera, and I'll ask the questions from here."

So much for my job. "What should I do?" I asked my mom.

"Hmm. This is a pretty simple setup. I don't know that there's much left."

I felt the disappointment settle in my stomach. "Okay. Can I take my video camera backstage and see what's there?"

"Great idea, Z! See if you can record some coverage shots. We may want to do some cutaways later underneath their voiceover, since this backdrop is so plain."

Real filming—yes! "I'm on it," I said, and felt my spirits lift. I went to grab my camera and helmet mount out of my backpack as I heard Mom introduce Amara.

I took a lap around the backstage area, filming the overflowing costume closet, a small group of kids running lines, and a shot of an enormous makeup kit. I also found a series of painted wooden signs backstage, which I panned across for a colorful shot.

I remembered how well my spontaneous interviews had fit into my CloudSong movie, so after I'd filmed everything backstage, I walked up to a group of campers.

"Hey, would you guys tell me a little bit about the camp?" I asked. "The movie is about how people are using new technology to connect and communicate."

"No wonder your mom wanted to come to Drama Connect, then," said Ellie, the girl playing Titania. "That's what the whole camp is about! Thanks to the live video streaming setup we have here, we can work with mentors from all over. Tomorrow we're all going to have a video chat visit with Ally Proctor. She's been on a couple of different kids' shows, and she's going to tell us about the business. How to get an agent, that kind of thing."

"That's really cool," I told her. "Do you have to apply or can you just sign up?"

Another girl spoke up. "You have to apply by submitting a video of yourself doing a scene. They have lots of scholarships, too, funded with money from donations and stuff. They want anyone who wants to come to have the chance."

"Like me," a tall girl with curly hair chimed in. "I've come here for the past four summers. But I could never have come without their scholarship program." She focused her eyes on my camera as she continued, "I'm going to be an instructor next year, actually. I can't wait to start giving back."

"Thanks for sharing that!" I looked around at the others. "So what's your favorite part about the camp?"

"Getting to act onstage all summer!" Ellie said, and everybody echoed their agreement.

After a few more questions, I waved good-bye to everyone and went back to the area in front of the stage. I figured the interview was probably almost over.

"Nice timing, Z," Mom said when I appeared. "Can you help me pack up my camera? Amara's going to get us a poster to shoot for an insert shot."

"Of course."

Mom started to follow Amara but then turned back. "Did you get anything good?"

"I think I did, yeah."

"Great, Z," Mom said. "I'm glad you thought of that."

We finished packing up our equipment and said good-bye to Amara and the campers, promising to be in touch.

"I wish I'd known about this place before," Nora said. "My niece Rebecca would love it. Maybe next summer. It's pretty far from Seattle, but maybe they have scholarships, or something."

"Oh no, the scholarships!" Mom exclaimed. "They definitely have them—I read about that in my prep work, and I could have sworn I had it in my notes to ask Amara about them, but I didn't. I can't believe no one brought that up. That angle really shows the community impact this camp is having, and that's such an important part of my vision for this film."

"Um, I have some footage about the scholarships," I said tentatively.

Mom was checking off items as we put them away. She looked up from her clipboard in surprise. "I thought you were getting B-roll shots backstage."

"Well, I did that, but it was a pretty small area, so

after that, I talked to some of the campers. I have footage of one of the older girls talking about how much the scholarships have meant to her."

"Z, that sounds like just what I need. Can I see the footage?"

We climbed into the RV. I rolled back what I'd shot on my camera and sat down beside Mom to show her. Nora sat on my other side to peek in, too. "This is perfect, Z!" Mom said.

"Second filming unit to the rescue!" Nora said, and gave me a high five.

I felt a little shy. "It was nothing. I just thought I should talk to the campers while I was back there."

"Well, good job," Mom said. "Now, let's go celebrate with some lunch."

"Excellent!" I agreed.

I settled in to relax as Mom maneuvered the RV out of its space. I pulled out my phone and was surprised to see that it had blown up while we were filming. I had eight messages from Mari. Oh no. Was something wrong back home?

I opened the first message, a video. It was Mari's band, Needles in a Haystack, onstage at the Beanery. Her mom must have filmed it. It seemed like a normal performance at first. But then I heard a familiar voice singing, and it wasn't the usual lead singer. "OMG!" I shouted out loud.

"What's going on back there?" Mom called.

"Mari sent me a video—Perry Carstairs from Chasing Wednesday jumped onstage with Needles in a Haystack today!" I called up to Mom. Chasing Wednesday was probably my favorite Seattle band. And I'd missed their lead singer jamming with Mari.

"I love Chasing Wednesday!" Nora said. "I saw them at the Crocodile last summer."

I tried to ignore Nora's comment. Of course she'd seen the band live, at one of the coolest spots in Seattle.

"Man, I can't believe I wasn't there," I said, shaking my head.

"But you're glad you were *here* today I hope?" Mom said. "Remember, *be in the now.* And you saved the day with your footage."

"I am glad!" I answered, and meant it. But why couldn't people be in two places at once? "I'm gonna go watch all the videos Mari sent me, and tell her congrats," I told Mom.

"Okay, Z. Tell her congratulations from me, too, okay?"

"I will," I promised. I curled up on the bed to watch the videos, cranking up the volume on my headphones and imagining I was there at the Beanery.

It really had been a great day of shooting.

But what a day to miss being back home!

Chapter 8

Overshare

The next morning, I loaded my camera into my backpack and went to help Mom and Nora divide up the equipment to carry into our interview. I knew from studying the binder last night that this company, Simulated Actuality (S/A for short), specialized in bringing virtual reality experiences to students of all ages.

"I've been meaning to tell you, I love your hat," Nora said, admiring my CREW cap.

"We'll have to get you one, too!" Mom said cheerfully as she handed Nora a camera case.

I tried not to groan out loud, and stepped forward to grab my own load.

"Z, I looked at some of the footage from Drama Connect last night. There were some great close-ups of the kids in the scene, and Nora said you took them. Great work."

"Thanks, Mom." I gave Nora a grateful smile, feeling guilty for not wanting her to have a CREW cap.

A man came forward and shook our hands when we walked in. "Hello, and welcome!" His T-shirt said: *Hi, I'm Josh. Ask me about S/A.*

We followed the very smiley and energetic Josh, who explained that he was the founder of S/A, from the lobby and into a room with the walls painted black. "This is one of our Virtual Reality Labs," he explained. "We find that having as blank a space as possible helps people really become immersed in the VR tech. Would you like to try out one of the headsets?"

"Absolutely!" Mom said. This was definitely her area. Mom was always talking about how VR was going to change the world someday.

I was busy scoping out all the cool things in the room. The walls may have been blank, but there was plenty of other stuff to look at! I half listened as Josh talked.

"Now, this tech is a prototype," he said. "A lot of what I'll show you today is—so no pictures, please. Our last stop will be our education gallery. We have some tech there that we use for larger groups.

That'll be your photo op, if you want to try to catch a funny shot."

I looked up from the visor I'd been inspecting. "I want a funny shot of my mom," I told Josh with a grin.

Mom's face basically said, *Absolutely not*. I gave her an innocent look.

"Ready to give it a try?" he asked. Mom grinned, and Josh helped her put a large black visor over her eyes. "You two will be able to see what Michelle is seeing up on this video monitor." Josh pulled a remote out of his pocket and pushed a button. A huge flat screen embedded in one of the black walls was suddenly visible.

Mom started walking forward, raising one hand in front of her, which looked pretty funny, since it was just a normal room. On the screen we saw a dense jungle, with plants everywhere. No wonder Mom was putting her hands up in front of her! She probably felt like she needed a giant machete to walk.

A tiger appeared in the jungle. No big deal—to us—but Mom squealed in surprise. Nora caught my eye and grinned. I forgot for a second that I wasn't a Nora fan and grinned back.

Mom kept walking through the simulation. A parrot came and landed on her shoulder; a monkey blocked her path. Then the demonstration was over, and Josh helped her pull the visor from her head.

"There," she said. "I didn't look that funny, did I?"

"Nope, not at *all*," I said in an exaggerated tone, and Mom and Nora both laughed.

We followed Josh into the next room, which he called the workshop.

"These are some of our most cutting-edge pieces of tech. We're working on refining the interface experience so that it's as seamless as possible." He handed Mom what looked like two oversize black gloves. "These are next-generation touch controllers. They're five times more reactive than the current industry standard, and they're also wireless. Take a look at the monitor," he told us. Mom had put the gloves on and was donning another visor. The screen showed what looked like a drone lying on a table, with a hatch open. Mom picked up one of the instruments that lay on the smaller table beside the drone, and when she tentatively poked with it, one of the drone's propellers spun. Mom jumped.

This was so cool! It definitely qualified as a

#summeradventure. I snapped a few shots with my phone, showing how engaged everyone was. Nora and Josh were watching the screen intently. I also recorded a few seconds of Mom "operating" on the drone and sent it all to my friends.

> **z:** Check out this amazing stuff, you guys! It's from this cool place called Simulated Actuality.

Becka texted right back:

> **BECKA:** This is so cool!

I shot back:

> **z:** Tx! Even more to come so stay tuned.

The final stop was the education gallery, where Nora and I finally got to try out headsets of our own. It was our photo op moment, and I took a few selfies with the VR visor on. This was going to make a perfect #summeradventure post.

Z On Location

We set up there for the interview with Josh. It was a pretty simple shoot with just one subject, and Mom was using only one camera. Nora was handling the mics and sound recording now, so I didn't have much to do. I sat on the floor in the back of the room and started to compose my post for later. I'd use my selfies and the other pics I'd gotten from the education gallery photo op to fill it out, adding hashtags for #summeradventure and #virtualreality. This was going to be my first really excellent post of the road trip, and I was hoping for lots of reposts and likes. Maybe this post would be the one that would grab Winter Costello's attention, and she'd give me a shout-out on one of her next vlogs.

We packed up the set in record time and arranged a time with Josh to come the next day to see a group of students interacting with the different interfaces. As we walked out, Mom reminded me, "I'm having dinner with Meg tonight—remember her, Z? We used to work together. So you two are on your own. Nora, I've got some cash for you if you don't mind taking Z out."

"Of course not. It'll be fun!"

It took maximum effort for me to avoid rolling my

eyes. I pretended to be looking up at the clouds instead. "Sure, great," I echoed.

"I know the perfect place," Nora told me. "I eat there every time I come to San Fran. And it's just a couple of blocks away."

I followed Nora, whose idea of a couple was apparently *eight*, because that's how many blocks it was.

"What is this place?" I asked when we got there. The sign outside the restaurant had a bunch of dancing vegetables and said THE CHEERFUL ONION.

"It's amazing—and everything's vegan!"

Ugh. Not exactly my idea of amazing.

Nora had already stepped inside The Cheerful Onion, so there didn't seem to be a way out.

The menu was decorated with a lot more dancing vegetables. "So what's good here?" I asked, settling in to the booth, and then had to work really hard not to fall asleep while Nora droned on about the different types of tofu.

I read through the menu, craving cheeseburgers and mac and cheese. But not with *vegan* cheese.

"How long have you been a vegan?" I asked her.

"Two years," Nora answered. Then, luckily, her phone dinged, so I didn't feel bad about checking my own.

The first thing I checked was Winter Costello's account. She'd posted several of her own #summer-adventure things from the day, and even reposted some of her followers' photos. I hoped that when she saw my post later tonight—after Mom's signoff, of course—that she'd repost it . . . that would get a *lot* more likes.

The food arrived pretty quickly. Nora attacked her Black Bean Celebration pizza, but I did more moving my food around my plate than actual eating. My Chickun Fiesta wrap had a weird consistency, sort of spongy and rubbery. I thought longingly of the bag of marshmallows back at the RV.

Nora's phone rang then, and she put her fork down quickly to answer it.

"Hi, Michelle, what's . . . ?"

Why was Mom calling? Her dinner with her friend couldn't be over yet.

I watched Nora's face for clues, but she didn't give anything away. "I understand," she said. "We'll be right there." I felt a sense of dread like a ball of ice in my stomach.

Nora grabbed some cash out of her bag and put it on the table. "We have to get back to the RV."

"What's going on?" I asked her as I followed her out. "Is Mom okay?"

"I'll let her explain it when we get there. I mean— yes, she's okay. But let's just walk fast now, huh?"

The knot of worry in my gut pulled tighter.

When we got to the RV, Nora opened the door for me to walk in, but I noticed that she didn't follow me.

Then I caught sight of my mom, who looked angrier than I'd ever seen her.

"Sit down, Z." Mom gestured to the table. "We need to talk about earlier today."

I took a seat, my heart pounding. What was I in trouble for?

"Josh Feldman called just a little while ago. He was letting me know that we are no longer welcome back at S/A tomorrow, as we'd planned, and he's revoked permission to use the interview footage from today. He's furious that someone posted video of their next-generation VR tech after he expressly asked us not to. He saw it on a random photo feed, because they tagged it with *the company*." Mom crossed her arms and shook her head. "Z, I'm at a complete loss here. Did you take videos when Josh said not to and then send them out?"

But I hadn't posted anything from today yet. Oh no. Becka or one of my other friends must have posted them and tagged me. I guess I never told them not to. This was totally my fault.

"After everything we just talked about, about not just sharing exciting things online, for you to do this . . ."

The ice ball in my stomach had spread to my limbs. I felt sick. I remembered Josh saying no pictures, but I thought he meant not to post them. I thought it would be okay to just share with my friends. All I really wanted to do was show them I was having the best #summeradventure. I should have told my friends not to post the photos. Or I guess I never should have sent them at all. All the other times I'd messed up on this trip were nothing compared to this. Now I could have caused some serious damage to Mom's reputation. I took a deep breath. "Mom, I'm *so* sorry . . ." I began, but then I didn't know what to say after that.

Mom put her hand up as though to stop me, even though I'd already fallen silent. "I hear that from you practically every day on this trip, Z. I'm actually too angry to hear any more right now. Angry and disappointed. But here's what's going to happen. Meg was there when I heard from Josh, and she had an idea for an alternate site to film tomorrow. It's all set up. However, you will stay in the RV. You will not be using your phone or your laptop. If it weren't for the fact that your friends are all meeting us at VidCon, you'd be going home tomorrow. Now, get ready for bed."

I nodded, feeling empty and hollow, and not just from hunger. "I should tell my friends to delete . . ."

"What's done is done," Mom said. Her expression softened. "Do you want to talk to Dad? You can use my phone for a video chat, if you want, before you go to bed."

I shook my head, still silent. I knew Mom would have already talked to him, and seeing one more disappointed parent face would definitely make me start crying. I handed Mom my phone and headed to the back of the RV.

After brushing my teeth and changing into pajamas, I crawled into bed and found a book I'd packed at the bottom of my bag, distantly remembering that when I brought it I'd thought that I wouldn't have time to read it. That I'd be too busy having my summer adventure. I opened the book, but I couldn't concentrate.

I closed the book and glanced at my laptop. Just

then, Mom came in wearing her pajamas. We were getting an early start the next day.

"I know you said no computer," I said, "but I want to write an e-mail to Josh. Apologizing. Can I do that now?"

Mom looked at me thoughtfully for a moment before answering. "I think that would be a good idea. But are you sure you wouldn't rather compose it in the morning after you've had some sleep?"

I shook my head. "I'd like to get it done now if it's okay."

"All right, go ahead and write it, then send it to me. I'll let you know if I see anything you need to change, and then I'll send it on to Josh for you."

"Okay. Thank you."

The e-mail was hard to write, and I struggled over the first few sentences, typing things and then deleting them over and over and over. Finally, I came up with a letter that seemed okay, and I sent it to Mom.

When I got back to bed, Mom's breathing was even. She'd fallen asleep. I closed my eyes and tried to do the same.

But as I lay there, I remembered the very worst part

of all. I now knew for a fact that I'd just lost my chance to interview Winter Costello. Mom hadn't mentioned it, but there was no way she'd let me do that now. I probably wouldn't even be allowed to be there for the interview.

I curled up but couldn't sleep. My brain just kept cycling back to all the ways I'd messed up Mom's film. There was so much more to think about on a professional shoot than the films I was used to making. Maybe I wasn't cut out to be a real filmmaker. Every time I thought I was getting it—I was wrong. And instead of getting better at things, I was messing up more and more. I really wished I could talk to my friends right now. I needed them more than ever, even though they'd probably be mad at me, too, for promising I'd try to get them into the interview with Winter when now I definitely wasn't going to do that.

Mom started to snore. I nudged her lightly and she rolled over. Lying there in the silence, I worried about my mom, and her film. I knew I was on the trip of a lifetime, learning about filmmaking firsthand from someone who really knew her stuff, but what if my mistakes totally ruined it for her? Would it turn out okay without the footage from Simulated Actuality? What if . . .

Mom let out another snore, snapping me out of my thoughts. I reached for a pair of earplugs, closed my eyes, and tried to fall asleep. I needed to get some rest—I had to be the best me tomorrow.

Chapter 9

Reboot

I woke up early the next morning, ready to get to work fixing the mess I'd made of this trip. The only problem was I couldn't do my *real* work since I was currently banned from the next shoot, but I'd never let a challenge stop me before.

Nora was already awake and sitting at the table. "Hey," I said.

"Morning," Nora replied.

"Hey, Nora—I'm really sorry I messed up the shoot." I waited for her response.

"Thanks for saying that. It's disappointing that we can't use the interview we got yesterday. But you don't need to apologize to me," she said gently. "Here, have a seat—how about if I make you some cocoa?"

I felt a rush of gratitude. I knew I 100 percent had not earned Nora's generosity. I shook my head. "Nope. I mean, thank you—but I'm going to help *you guys* today. Do you want some coffee?"

Nora blinked in surprise but said, "Sure. I'll take hazelnut."

I grabbed the box of coffee pods from the cabinet and measured out the water. I pulled down the toaster, too, and plugged it in before I opened the bag of English muffins.

As I made breakfast, Nora said, "Can I ask, Z—why *did* you share that footage?"

She sounded genuinely curious. And kind. So I answered honestly. "I knew he said no pictures, but I guess I thought he meant not to post them online. I really thought it would be okay to share them with my friends. I just got so caught up in the excitement, and was just thinking of finally having something awesome to send them. Now I see how silly that was." I paused, not sure if I was ready to open up and tell Nora everything that was on my mind. Still, she looked at me with more concern and interest than she had shown the whole rest of the trip, so I went on. "Right before we left, Winter Costello, who's basically my online idol, started the hashtag #summeradventure, and I was so psyched to participate. But being an assistant has been way harder than I thought, and yesterday seemed like my first chance for a really great post. I was just planning to use something from the end—the photo op. But I wanted to give my friends a preview, to show them what an amazing experience yesterday was. They all seem to be having really awesome summers."

"That makes sense," Nora said. "When I first started college, I wanted to share everything with everyone. But the stuff I posted was boring to everyone I knew, since I'm from Seattle and stayed there for school. But almost everyone I knew went *away* to college. I had a friend who went to school in New York City, and even one who went to Edinburgh, in Scotland. She kept posting pictures of castles—it looked like she'd gotten to go to Hogwarts," Nora added with a laugh.

I laughed, too. "You must have been jealous."

"I was, but then things kind of evened out. I'm a film student, you know, so my homework is sometimes to make a movie, which is pretty cool. My friend in Scotland was studying medieval literature—so once she ran out of castle selfies, there wasn't that much to post. Plus, remember, everybody only posts their own highlights. You can't measure your everyday against their highlight reel."

"That's very film student-y advice," I told her. "I'll try to remember that, if I'm ever allowed online again. For now, you want an English muffin?"

"Sure," Nora said.

"Nora, can you think of any other way I can help today? Other than breakfast?" I turned around and leaned against the little counter, hoping Nora's nice streak would continue.

"I'm not sure," Nora said. "Your mom made it pretty clear that you were to stay here during today's shoot."

I knew Nora was right, but maybe there was some way I could be helpful. "Is there something I could do that wouldn't require me leaving the RV?" I asked Nora. She looked around and thought for a moment.

"Actually, I do have an idea for you. What about handling the equipment inventory before and after the shoot? It's not glamorous, but you wouldn't have to actually go to the shoot to do it . . ."

"No—I mean, that's a great idea! Do you think Mom would let me do that?"

"My advice? Just jump in with the precheck and see."

I nodded gratefully. "Thanks."

"No problem. I'll go get the precheck clipboard, and

we can start on that while we eat. You'll impress your Mom right away this morning," Nora said.

"Thanks, Nora." I put her English muffin in the toaster and pressed the lever, thinking that she wasn't so bad after all.

By the time Mom was ready for breakfast twenty minutes later, Nora had helped me with the full pre-check inventory, and I had Mom's French vanilla coffee pod all ready to go. I hit BREW and stood beside the machine, waiting to bring her the mug.

"Thank you, Z," Mom said when I gave her the coffee.

I handed her the clipboard, too. "I was hoping I could help with the inventory. I know I can't come on the shoot today, but I still want to help. If it's okay."

Mom scanned the clipboard. "This looks good, Z." She studied my face, then seemed to come to a decision. "You can handle this job for the rest of the trip. Good thinking."

She sounded just a little warmer this morning. I knew she'd forgive me eventually, but I was going to have to work really hard for it to be sooner rather than later. "Okay. Thanks, Mom."

"We'll be back around one thirty, and we'll go get a late lunch with you." She handed me my phone back. "Don't get too excited. This is for safety, in case you have to call us. I've enabled the parent control app, and put it on the emergency contacts calls only setting."

My heart sunk hearing that Mom thought she needed to do that. But I'd just shown her yesterday that she couldn't trust me. I knew it was up to me to prove to her, again, that she could.

"Okay," I said as I took the phone.

"We're going to be just down the block," Mom continued. "I wrote the address down for you." She handed me a piece of paper with an address and a hand-drawn map. "But unless there's an emergency, we'll see you after the shoot."

I nodded and stood on the steps of the RV as they left, loaded down with gear—even more so than usual without me to carry some of it.

I tried passing the time by making a storyboard for a new stop-motion video, but I just couldn't concentrate.

I knew I couldn't just sit around the RV all morning,

though. I tidied up the common area a little and ran across the trip binder that Mom had made—the one that held all the information about the equipment she was using on the project.

Suddenly, it hit me, and I don't know why I didn't think of it before. Mom already knew how to use all this stuff. And at the start, she hadn't known Nora would be coming along. The only reason Mom had compiled all that info and written all those notes was for me. And when I was supposed to be studying it, I'd been too focused on the world inside my phone, rather than the real world right in front of me, just like Mom had said.

I'd really messed up—and not just by sharing the VR tech.

But my parents had always taught me that if you mess up, you keep going. It was time to start the trip over—time to come back from my crash with a full Z reboot.

I opened the binder to the page about camera setup and pulled out Mom's backup camera, then practiced getting it on the tripod and adjusting the settings for a typical interview. When it was all set up, I put it away in the bag and started over again. After a few tries, my timing was really improving.

Before I knew it, Mom and Nora were back. I jumped into action inventorying the equipment, double-checking everything carefully before making a note on the clipboard. Then I used the special lens-cleaning wipes before putting all the lenses back in their cases. Mom saw what I was doing and gave me a small nod.

Once I'd done everything I could think of with the equipment, I went back to studying the binder. Tomorrow was VidCon. I thought back to the beginning of the trip, when I'd been so excited to go to VidCon, and I'd been sure I'd be interviewing Winter there. Even though I had blown my chance at that, I was still psyched to meet up with Becka, Gigi, and Mari—they always made me feel like I could do anything and no challenge was too big. They were my real-life crew, and exploring VidCon with them was surely going to feel like a real adventure. We had a huge list of panels we wanted to attend and stuff we wanted to see.

But for now, I had a long while in the RV before we got there. I planned to use the time reading Mom's binder cover to cover. Maybe I wouldn't get another chance to be Mom's assistant on this trip. But at least I could use this time to learn how to use all this stuff.

It could be my own mini film camp, which was *almost* a #summeradventure.

Mom parked the RV in one of the oversize spaces at the convention center. I had packed up the equipment and put it on the table, ready to go. We all loaded up, but before we headed out, mom held out my phone.

I looked up at her in surprise. "Are you giving this back?"

"Phone and text only. Okay?"

"Okay!" I said, sitting up straighter and accepting the phone from her.

"I've been noticing your behavior," Mom added. "Just keep it up. I really want to trust you again."

"I want you to, too. Can I text Mari, Becka, and Gigi about meeting up?" I asked.

"Sure, " Mom replied. "Tell them to meet us at the east entrance."

It ended up being a looonnng walk from our parking space. "This is the glamorous side of filmmaking," Mom joked as she hitched her bag higher on her shoulder.

I ran ahead a little, anxious to get my first look at VidCon—and my friends. Mari came barreling at me as soon as I entered—and almost knocked me over, since I was holding so much equipment. "Z, you're finally here—I can't *wait* to tell you all about Perry Carstairs and Chasing Wednesday! Can you even believe that he came up onstage with us? I'm still dying."

"I'm dying that I missed it," I told her. "Here, do you mind carrying this one?" I handed her a heavy bag.

"Sure. So you watched the videos I sent, right? I'm still pinching myself."

Mari kept on chattering about Chasing Wednesday. "It was so crazy meeting them, but you getting to interview Winter will be out of this world amazing!" Mari said.

I gulped. I had to fess up about what happened, but I wanted to wait until Becka and Gigi got here.

"What's up with you? You're being really quiet," Mari said.

"I'm still bummed I missed your big moment. But there's also something I want to talk to you about. With everyone."

"Hi, Mari," Mom called as she and Nora caught up. "This is Nora, my assistant."

"Hi, Nora," Mari said. "It's nice to meet you." She raised her eyebrows at me—I hadn't mentioned Nora.

Just then, I heard a squeal, and Becka and Gigi exploded out of the elevator and headed toward us. Mari and I hugged them both; it was so good to see them in person after a whole year.

"I'm can't believe we're finally here!" Gigi said. "It seems like I've been counting the days forever."

"Just since three hundred sixty-four days ago," Becka joked. "We're back where it all started!"

Mom stepped forward and greeted the two new-comers, and introduced Nora to them as well.

"You girls have a plan of attack for your second year at VidCon?"

"We sure do," Becka told her. "The only trouble is for some time slots, I have two or three panels I want to see!"

"Let's get started," Mari said. "Or do you have to film today?" she asked me.

"We've got this covered," Mom said, and I sent her a silent thank-you for not outing me. I was going to tell my friends about messing up and being benched as an assistant—but I definitely preferred to wait until we were on our own to do so.

Everyone agreed to help carry some equipment over to the room where Mom would be during her interview. I knew this was the biggest shoot of the whole film—Mom was doing a speed round of interviews with tech and digital innovators. As much as I wanted to hang out and explore with my friends, missing this shoot was really a bummer. This was completely unlike anything we'd done yet, and the pace would probably be even faster than usual. I wished I could watch Mom and Nora in action. I gave Mom a hug and said, "Good luck. If things get really hectic, text me and I'll come back to help."

I walked slowly behind Mari, Becka, and Gigi as we headed back to the main part of the convention floor.

"Are you okay?" Mari asked.

I gave a big sigh. "I have to tell you guys something. I messed up really badly, more than once, and I'm not really helping them on the shoots anymore."

"Speaking of *them*, who's this Nora person? I thought *you* were going to be your mom's assistant," Gigi said.

"I was." I told them everything from the beginning. When I came to the photo-sharing mistake, Becka said, "Oh my gosh, Z, that is all my fault! I was the one who posted the photo." It looked like Becka was about to cry, and I bent down to give her a hug.

"I take all the blame. I shouldn't have taken or sent the photos in the first place."

Becka wiped her eyes. "But if I hadn't . . ."

"What's done is done," I said.

"I feel like that could happen to anyone," Mari put in. "You just got excited about finding a summer adventure."

"Thanks, Mari. I was really just thinking about finding something great to post. I've realized I do that a lot."

"That happens to me sometimes, too," Gigi said. "A couple weeks ago, I went on a trip to Stonehenge with my school, and I feel like I totally missed out on learning about the history and all that, because I was basically only thinking about the pictures I could post!"

"Yeah, exactly. That's totally how I've been on this trip. Even before we left I was like *What can I post to win Winter's #summeradventure challenge?*"

Mari jumped in. "I had a little bit of that when Perry Carstairs was playing with us onstage. Like, half my brain was going: *OMG Perry Carstairs OMG, I can't believe this is happening, I wonder if his fans will see this online and then they'll see Needles in a Haystack and then we'll blow up and it will all be because of this thing that is happening RIGHT*

NOW . . . and the other half of my brain was like *Yeah, this is happening RIGHT NOW! Enjoy it!*"

I smiled at her, then said to the group, "There's one more thing. My mom told me before we left that I needed to prove myself in order to do the interview with Winter Costello. Obviously, that didn't happen. I know you guys were excited . . ."

"Say no more," Becka broke in. "I love Winter Costello, but there are so many other amazing people here this week. And I have a whole bunch of their names highlighted right here." She held up an already well-worn copy of the event program. "So I say, we're burning daylight here—let's get this show on the road!"

"I second that," Gigi said. "This is VidCon. Anything can happen! I mean, think about it: We all met right here, in this very place, one year ago. Can you believe it's only been a year? I feel like I've known you guys for ages."

"Anything can happen . . ." I echoed. The beginnings of an idea were teasing around the corners of my brain. "Becka, you said that you had some time slots when there were too many things to see happening all at once, right?"

Becka nodded. "I'd need a time machine to see everything."

"I have an idea. What if we check out the exhibit hall together first, but then each pick one of the panels Becka highlighted, and divide and conquer. We could split into pairs and film the different events—a live report from the scene type of thing. Then we can meet back up and share our stories." Winter Costello wasn't the only amazing online celebrity here. I'd find my own incredible story and get to work on a film about it. I wasn't allowed to use my phone, but I had my camera, and that was just straight filmmaking.

"Great plan, Z!" Gigi said.

"Sounds cool. Z's Crew reporting live from VidCon," Mari agreed.

"I'm in," Becka said. "But first, race you to the main exhibition hall!"

Becka took off at full speed, and we all laughed as we raced to catch up.

Chapter 10

Second Chances

We dove into Becka's highlighted schedule, and divided up the 1:00 p.m. panels. Kacey Kravitz—along with her adorable Roxie the Robot—was appearing at that time. I told my friends how great Kacey was, and then Gigi and Mari decided they wanted to go to the panel and meet her.

I told them to mention my name to Kacey. "Tell her I said hi and I hope I get to see her again on the floor, okay?"

"Sure thing, Z," Gigi said with a smile. "We'll tell Roxie, too."

We finished making our selections, and then it was time to head out to record our vlog stories.

Becka and I chose a panel that featured up-and-coming female vloggers under the age of twenty-five. When we got there, I saw a pretty long line, not unlike the one Lauren and Mari and I had been waiting in when we met Becka and Gigi last year. Becka went off to find a bathroom while I joined the line, got out my camera, and decided to ask some "on the fly" questions of the people standing near me. After all, doing person-on-the-street style interviews had worked out well for me with both my CloudSong movie and when I'd done them backstage at Drama Connect for Mom's film.

A trio of girls who looked to be about my age stood in front of me. I edged around to face them and prepared to introduce myself.

"Z?" One of the girls said before I even opened my mouth. "You're Z, aren't you?"

I felt my eyes widen in surprise. "Um . . . yes! But how did you know?"

"We're in Z's Crew!" another of the girls said. "I'm Jordyn. We *love* your AGSM videos!"

I stared at them in disbelief. "You guys subscribe to my channel?"

"Of course! Like Jordyn said, we're part of your crew!" the third girl said. "I'm Erica, and this is Mina." The first girl—Mina—waved.

"I can't believe you guys recognized me!" I said.

"So are you on this panel?" Erica asked, leafing through her program. "I didn't see your name . . ."

I felt my giant grin fade just a little. "No, unfortunately. But maybe someday!" I added brightly.

"For sure," said Mina.

"Totally," agreed Jordyn. "But, hey, guys we *have* to interview Z for our vlog!" She turned to the others, and they both nodded and agreed.

"We're just getting started," Mina said. "We don't have many followers yet. But we all love vlogging—would you want to do a chat in the Connectivity Café with us? Maybe this afternoon?"

I opened my mouth to say, "Of course!"—but then I remembered that I needed to meet back up with Mari and Gigi. I didn't want them to think I'd put doing an interview ahead of spending time with them.

"I'd love to, I really would. I have to meet back up with my friends after this panel, though . . ." Just then, Becka returned. I introduced her to my followers. I still couldn't believe they were real!

"You should totally come, too! Becka, do you help with Z's vlog?" Erica asked.

"My friends help me with all my projects," I said.

"Z's Crew forever!" Becka answered. Everyone laughed.

"Can we do the interview at four?" Erica asked.

"Sure!" I agreed. "Um, I was actually going to ask if I could interview *you* guys. I'm doing a video about this panel, and I want to add some comments from fans."

"Of course!" Jordyn said, and the others agreed. I asked them a few questions, but before we knew it, the line was moving and we were being let into the room to see the panel.

We sat with my new friends to listen to the vloggers. I imagined myself sitting up there on a panel like that one day. Then I remembered that Erica had actually been looking for my name on the list in her program. I felt a rush of happiness at the thought. Besides that, I'd just met *actual* fans of my channel. They recognized me. Sitting there as the panel ended, looking up at the stage, I felt absolutely sure that I'd get there someday. I just had to keep going. Filmmaking was hard work, but VidCon was super inspiring. I already had tons of ideas for vlogs. The sting of not getting to interview Winter was fading away.

After the panel, Becka and I said good-bye to the girls and headed toward the meeting spot my friends and I had picked.

I pulled my phone out of my pocket to see if any of them had texted me, but at that moment, it chimed with a phone call—from Mom.

"Mom!" I said, picking up the phone. "You'll never guess what . . ."

"Hold on, Z—can you tell me about it later? I need you to get back here ASAP."

"Oh—is everything okay?"

"Not really. Nora isn't feeling well at all. She thinks it's food poisoning from that veggie burger she had last night. At any rate, I sent her back to the RV. She's in no shape to help me . . . and I can't do this by myself, not this shoot. I really need your help, Z."

My heart was pounding. Mom was asking me to help her with the shoot. Sure, it was because Nora was sick, but still . . . "Z? Are you there?"

"Sorry! Yes—I'm coming. I'll be right there!"

I hung up and headed back the way I'd come.

Mom needed my help! And I'd get to at least *participate* in the shoot with Winter, after all.

"Becka, I have to go help my mom. Nora's sick. Can you meet up with Mari and Gigi and let them know what's going on?"

"Sure! I hope everything's okay. We'll meet you at the Connectivity Café at four. Just text if there's a problem. Good luck!"

Oh no. Four o'clock was when I was supposed to

meet Erica, Mina, and Jordyn. What if I was late? Or couldn't make it at all? I didn't want them to think I'd blown them off. Hopefully, if I didn't make it, Becka could explain to them, and they'd understand.

All thoughts of trying to explain my dilemma to Mom evaporated as soon as I entered the room where she was doing her interviews. The scene was chaotic. I guess in the rush to help Nora, setup had gotten way behind schedule. Mom looked up from positioning a camera and caught my eye, and she looked incredibly relieved to see me, as though I were a human life preserver.

Whatever I had to do to help her, I'd do it. Maybe if I was the best possible assistant, we could get finished early so I could get to the Connectivity Café on time.

I walked up to Mom. "What do you need?"

I set up the B camera in record time. My practice with the backup camera had really paid off.

"What next?" I asked Mom.

"Did you set that up already?"

"Yes, and the key light."

Mom raised an eyebrow at me and walked over to the camera to check its settings. Then her eyebrow climbed higher. "Perfect. Okay, why don't you unpack the lavalier mics?"

"I already have them set up," I said, gesturing to a small table a few feet away. "Is it okay if I ask our subject to do a sound check with me? She's waiting right there— I got her a water bottle from your cooler when she came in."

Mom's eyes widened a bit and she nodded. "I'll just go greet her and ask her if she's ready for a sound check." Mom started to walk away and then turned back. "Really good work, Z." I felt a small jump of joy in my chest. *There's more to be done,* I told myself. *Stay focused.*

Once everything was set up, we began the series of interviews. I ran the B camera, and Mom ran the A and asked the questions. The first subject, Ann Weymouth, was very quiet; Mom had a hard time getting her to say very much. She was a genius gaming programmer, but it seemed like she was probably more comfortable with computers than being in the spotlight. I noticed she had a key chain on her bag that said I LOVE MY YORKIE, and while Mom changed her camera setup partway through, I showed Ann pictures of Popcorn from my phone. I knew it wasn't texting or calling, but I figured opening my camera roll in the name of relaxing the interview subject would be okay.

"She's at least six of my Peanut!" Ann exclaimed. "But she's so adorable. Is she licking the camera there?"

I sighed. "Yes, Popcorn always wants to check to see if *everything* is edible."

"Peanut's the opposite. She's a very picky eater."

Ann had to stop telling me about the complicated process of figuring out what Peanut would eat in order to finish the interview. She was much more talkative answering the second round of questions. Once we said good-bye to Ann, it was time to set up for the next subjects. Since there were two, we'd need to change the arrangement a bit.

"I'm not sure what you said to Ann, but you really got her talking," Mom said.

I shrugged. "I saw her dog key chain, so I showed her some pictures of Popcorn. I hope that's okay. We bonded over dog-loving."

"Yes, it's okay, in this case. Sometimes getting the subject to talk is the hardest part of the interview."

We got everything reset and the next three interviews passed in a whirlwind. I kept my ears open for

any instructions from Mom, but I also tried to antici-
pate what she might need. I was beginning to realize
that being a good assistant was kind of a balancing
act. It wasn't just about helping to set up and break
down, it was about supporting the whole shoot. Like I
knew one of Mom's subjects had just posted something
new she was working on, so I made sure Mom knew
to ask about that instead of just jumping in and asking myself. But sometimes jumping in *was* necessary,
like when I made Ann a bit more comfortable. I thought
I understood now why Mom had warned me about
distractions on set. The balancing act took a lot of
concentration.

It took so much concentration that I didn't even
think about the fact that I might miss the meet-up at the
Connectivity Café at 4 p.m. The first four interviews
went smoothly and before I knew it, it was already 3:40.

"Our final subject is here, Z," Mom said.

I turned to greet her and realized that I'd been so
focused on being the best assistant ever, I'd also forgotten that the last interview subject was Winter Costello!
How could I have forgotten *that*?

"Z," Mom was saying, "meet Winter Costello.

Winter, this is my daughter, Z, who's also my assistant today. She's a big fan of yours."

"It's always nice to meet a fan," Winter said with a big smile, and held out her hand to shake mine. She'd added some dark blue at the tips of her hair, and she looked so cool.

"I . . . it's so amazing to see you in person instead of on my screen! I have been posting all my summer adventures. Well, not all." Mom gave me a little smile.

"That's awesome," Winter said. "It's been really fun to see what everyone is up to."

Mom showed Winter where she'd be sitting for the interview. I stood staring after her, starstruck, for a few moments, then shook myself to get back to work, and went to get the lavalier mic for Winter.

Mom returned to stand beside me. "Z, you've really done an outstanding job today. I can tell that you've been studying."

"I have," I answered. "I really wanted to show you I could do this."

"I knew you could. You just had to learn to be present in the moment."

"Boy, were you right."

Mom smiled. "I'm your mom. I know these things.

But, listen, Z—after the interview, Winter has agreed to let you do a mini interview. She'll have time for you to ask three or four questions. I thought you could use the footage for your vlog."

I felt my heart swell with joy. "Oh, Mom! Really?? I would love . . ." My heart sank.

"I can't."

"What do you mean?"

Briefly, I told her about meeting my followers, and agreeing to do the interview for *their* vlog. "I was going to tell you about it when I got here, but there wasn't time." I took a deep breath and let it out. "I want to do that interview with Winter more than anything . . ."

I knew that an interview with someone so famous and impressive would give my own vlog tons of exposure. But this wasn't just about likes for my vlog. I'd given my word to Erica, Mina, and Jordyn. My IRL Z's Crew. I had to be in the now.

"I want to—so much. But I need to keep my promise. Is it okay if I help you finish the setup and then go meet the girls from Z's Crew?"

Mom nodded. "Of course. I think it's the right thing to do." She looked at her watch. "All we have left to do is set up Winter's mic, actually. I can do that. You go meet your fans and I'll meet you back here to tear down the setup. Say, five o'clock?"

"Okay. Thanks, Mom!" I gave her a quick hug.

Then I raced toward the Connectivity Café. I had to make it in time.

Chapter 11

Girl Power

I hoped I wasn't too late to meet my fans. I skidded around the corner into the hallway that led to the café, out of breath and ready to scan the crowd to find the three girls I was meeting.

The café was completely full, and when I rounded the corner, almost everyone there started cheering.

Mari, Becka, and Gigi rushed forward to greet me. Erica appeared beside them. "We spread the word!" she said, beaming.

"Wait—do you mean—is everyone here for *me*?"

I saw Mina and Jordyn come up behind Erica. "Yep, it turns out there are lots of members of Z's Crew here at VidCon!" Mina said.

I looked around in amazement. There had to be almost fifty people in the room. "You're kidding."

"Nope," Jordyn said. "Hey, everyone. Let's welcome Z!"

Everyone shouted, "Hi, Z!"

"I thought I might have missed you guys," I said, still dazed at the number of people who'd turned up.

What if I hadn't come? I felt sick for a second, considering the idea, but then I shook it off. I had made the right choice. Now I could just enjoy the interview, and the chance to meet so many members of the crew in real life.

"Come this way, Z," Erica said. "We're going to use Jordyn's laptop to record. Sorry we're so low-tech."

"It's not the tech, it's how you use it," I told her.

"I'm writing that down," said a girl with very blonde hair who was beside me. She was carrying a small notebook and writing as she walked.

"Wow, are you really writing that down?" I asked her. "I feel so famous."

"You are. I watch *all* your videos. I've been watching since you started. I'm Amy, by the way."

"Nice to meet you, Amy. I'm Z. But . . . I guess you knew that," I added, feeling embarrassed. I'd always wanted to be recognized for my films. It turned out it was just a little bit awkward. But I didn't really mind so much.

"Here's the seat we have ready for you," Mina said.

"You really should interview Mari, Gigi, and Becka, too," I said. "I couldn't have done any of my projects without their input. And my friend Lauren also helps, but she's at soccer camp," I added.

"That'd be great, but I only brought one mic . . ." Jordyn held it up with a frown.

I shrugged. "Oh, hey—no worries—we'll just pass it among us. We'll try not to talk over each other like we usually do!"

Mina was setting up two more chairs beside mine, and Mari jumped in to help find a spot for Becka's wheelchair.

Before I knew it, the interview had started. A hush fell over the café as Erica asked us to introduce ourselves, then went on to the first question. "So, Z, can you tell us how you got started making stop-motion movies?"

I explained about my mom being a film professor and filmmaker. "I've wanted to make movies for as long as I can remember, and I've always loved my AG dolls. This way I could combine two things I love. My favorite part is getting to share my vision of the world with the audience."

"How do your friends help you?"

"I'm Z's fashion consultant," Mari said. "Our friend Lauren helps out with a lot of the props."

"I guess Gigi and I are the critics," Becka said. "I remember the first time we told you our opinion of your CloudSong film. You weren't too happy with us, I don't think."

I felt a flash of embarrassment, but then I decided to own it. Becka was right. "Becka and Gigi are always honest with me about my filmmaking. They tell me what's working—and what isn't. I think it's really important to have a support system of friends who'll give you their real opinion. Not just what they think you want to hear."

"Is that the toughest part about being a filmmaker?" Erica asked.

I was shaking my head before I'd even thought about how to answer. I knew that what I'd learned this summer was connected to Mom's advice: *Be in the now.* But it was more complicated than that. I wasn't even sure if I could explain.

"The hardest part for me, so far, isn't so much about the filmmaking—it's about the rest of my life around it.

I love having my own channel, and having followers means so much to me." I smiled gratefully at the crowd. "But it's also a lot of pressure. I was so excited to help my Mom with her documentary this summer, and to be part of making a real film." I took a deep breath. I was about to admit the not-so-glamorous part of my journey this summer.

Mom always said that in interviews, authenticity is key. So I told them everything. From forgetting to turn off my phone to dropping the mic. And even about posting pictures that cost my mom an interview. "Basically, you guys, I was a disaster. But the good news is, I learned a lot from everything that happened this summer. Every time I messed up, it was because I was so caught up in the online world or what I'd share *afterward* that I forgot to really be present right at that moment. And no matter how it might look online, getting to go on a filmmaking road trip with your mom is quite an adventure, all on its own."

We wrapped up the interview, and I thanked everyone for letting me share my experiences. It felt so awesome to really connect with all these people I had only known online. I looked out at the crowd, still amazed at how many fans had shown up for this interview. But I also saw someone I hadn't expected to see.

Mom was smiling at me, and when she caught my eye, she gave me a thumbs-up sign.

That's when I noticed that Winter Costello was standing right next to her.

Right after I saw her, the café erupted, as one member of Z's Crew whispered to the next that Winter Costello was standing *right there*. I knew everyone in the café would recognize Winter. I'd made a video about how much I looked up to her, and it had been one of my most-watched—and liked—posts.

Winter started to make her way up to where we were sitting, although she had to stop a few times to talk to fans.

"Hi there, Z," Winter said with a smile when she finally got to me.

"Hi, Winter!" I said. "I . . . What are you doing *here*?" I looked at Mom in confusion. Surely it wasn't anything she needed from me as an assistant. She wouldn't have brought Winter if that were the case.

"Your mom told me about your interview here. It sounded pretty interesting to me. You know, I'm putting together a VidCon edition of my Girl Power vlog. You meeting some of your followers here in real life sounded like a great interview opportunity."

I felt confused for a few seconds. But then it hit me. Winter was asking to interview *me*.

My mouth fell open in shock, and I struggled to think of what to say. "I'd . . . That would be amazing. But I guess I don't really get . . . why me?" Just the other day I'd been banned from shooting with Mom and Nora, a completely disgraced former film crew member. Today, everything was different.

"Z, look around. You connected with all of these girls by sharing something of yourself online: your ideas, your films. And you're here with your friends, your support system. It seems to me like this is pretty much the definition of girl power. So what do you say?"

"Say yes, Z!" Amy called, and everyone laughed.

"Go, Z!" someone else shouted, and then everyone was chanting it. My cheeks were on fire. I felt embarrassed and thrilled at the same time.

"I'm in," I told Winter.

"I'll film it for you," Mom said from the back of the room, hoisting her camera bag with a broad grin.

The interview went by in a blur. I kept thinking what an amazing compliment it was, for Winter to ask to interview *me*. I also realized that I was having the ultimate #summeradventure moment.

"What is the most important advice you can give to girls who are interested in filmmaking?" Winter asked me.

I glanced at Mom. "Be in the now. It's amazing to share what you love, and what you've experienced and learned, with friends and followers online. But it's also pretty easy to get too caught up in what you'll post and who will see it and like it, and then you can forget to really be present for the actual event."

"That's excellent advice," Winter said. "It's actually a really great perspective for me to keep in mind. The virtual world is awesome, but we have to keep one foot in this world, don't we?"

We talked for a while about how stop-motion works, and what new kinds of things I was going to do. I had so many ideas just from being around all these amazing people at VidCon. I was bubbling over with excitement.

Everyone laughed at how enthusiastic I sounded. Then Winter was saying, "Thank you, Z, for being with me here today at VidCon." I saw Mom lower her camera, and I knew the interview was finished.

I sat there dazed as Winter shook my hand. She handed me a business card and then went to talk to Mom for a few seconds. Then she was gone.

"Oh, man—I should have gotten her autograph!" Becka said. "It all happened so fast."

"Z just got interviewed by *Winter Costello*," Mari said.

"It was brilliant!" Gigi exclaimed.

"Thanks," I said. "It was kind of nerve-racking, but it felt incredible." That was not how I meant to get on Winter's vlog—and I didn't even have to have "the best" #summeradventure, I just had to be myself. And that was about a thousand times better.

"I'm so jealous," Becka said.

"Me, too," Gigi said.

"I hope somebody recorded that on their phone," I said to my friends. "We *have* to text Lauren."

"On it!" Mari said.

Mom came over to join us. "What was Winter saying to you?" I asked her.

"I was letting her know that I'd send her the footage I just took. I'm really proud of you—how you turned things around on this trip."

"I guess I made a comeback," I agreed.

"A comeback makes for a better adventure story than being perfect from the start anyway," Becka told me with a smile.

Becka always gave the best story advice, so she was probably right.

Amy, the girl with the notebook, came up to me then. "Some of us were wondering what you were doing now. We thought maybe we could check out some of the booths together, if you wanted?"

"Can I?" I asked Mom, and she nodded. "That sounds amazing to me," I told Amy. I stood up on my chair to make myself a little taller. "Attention! We're going to check out the exhibition floor, if anyone wants to join us."

"When?" someone called.

"Right now. Z's Crew—let's head out!"

Chapter 12

The Best Kind

Nora seemed to be feeling better when we got back to the RV. She was packing up her stuff since she'd left her car in San Francisco and would be leaving us here. "Hey, superstar. I heard about your interview."

"News travels fast, I guess!" Mom smiled at us and stepped outside to call Dad. We were going to pack up and hit the road first thing in the morning. I couldn't believe how amazing my #summeradventure was. I thought about all I had learned over the past week, and realized that I had learned a lot from Nora, too. I guess we had more in common than I wanted to admit. I sat down at the little table.

"Nora, I'm really glad I met you. I wasn't exactly excited when you first came. I guess you could probably tell. But now . . ."

"I could tell." Nora laughed. "But I understand. You were expecting to have your mom all to yourself."

"It was more like I thought I could be the ultimate assistant all by myself. But Mom was right. I wasn't ready. I know I'm getting closer, though. I learned so much from watching Mom. And you."

"Aw, thanks, Z. That means a lot to me. I'm still learning, too, so sometimes I forget how much I already know! I don't think that ever stops."

"Hopefully we'll see each other again," I said. "But if we go out to a restaurant, can it not be *entirely* vegan?"

Nora laughed. "I knew you didn't like The Cheerful Onion! Okay, deal. Someplace with veggie *and* beef burgers." Nora gave me a hug. "Speaking of veggie burgers," she said, "I'd never say I was exactly happy to have food poisoning, but I'm glad something good came of it. And you totally stepped up." She held her fist up for a bump. "Girl power!"

I laughed and bumped her fist. "Thanks, Nora. I'm glad you're feeling better, though."

We decided to eat the rest of the snacks in the RV for dinner. While I was slurping Cup Noodles, Lauren texted me.

LAUREN: OMG Just saw the interview! I can't wait to hear all about it!

I texted back.

Z: Can't wait to hear about camp, too! Let's meet up at the Beanery as soon as we get home. I'm dying for a bubble tea!

I turned my phone off so I could enjoy the last night with my mom and Nora on the road.

The next morning, we drove Nora back to the airport where she said good-bye to Mom, and waved to me. "See you later, Z!"

"Thank you again, Nora," Mom told her. "You're a lifesaver. I'll see you in Advanced Concepts in August, right?"

"I'll be in the front row."

"Yes, thank you, Nora!" I called as she went down the steps.

Mom turned to me. "You and Nora seem to have bonded at last."

I nodded. "We did. Nora's really smart. I can see why you picked her to come with us."

"She is pretty great, but I have to say I'm a little surprised to hear you say so." Mom put the RV into reverse, and I sat in the passenger's seat and buckled my seat belt.

"Well . . . I had to get past what I expected the trip to be like so I could appreciate what it actually was. Which got a lot easier when Z's Crew showed up at VidCon! And when Winter Costello asked to interview me!"

"Yes, all of that probably helped with your enjoyment just a *little* bit."

"Seriously, though—thanks, Mom. This has been an amazing trip. I learned so much, both about making films and about being in the moment."

"I'm glad to hear you say that."

"I think it's always going to be hard, though," I told her. "I've been thinking about it a lot, and realized that, for me, sharing online is almost like part of the experience. If I don't get to share it later, it's kind of like it didn't completely happen. Does that make sense to you?"

"Not completely. But remember, we didn't post and share back in ye olden times when I was growing up."

"I know." I laughed. "Speaking of posting and sharing, I really wanted to do one more vlog from the road. I'm feeling kind of inspired. Do you mind?"

"Of course not. But after this, we are officially on vacation. No more vlogging, okay?" Mom said.

"Sounds like a plan," I said, pulling out my laptop.

It felt like years ago that we set out on this trip, and it had been so much more than just a #summeradventure. I had hoped to learn a lot of new filmmaking skills, but I had learned way more than that.

I flipped open my laptop and turned on the video camera. Sometimes I wrote up a script for myself, and sometimes I had notes. But today I felt like just going off-the-cuff.

"Hey, Z's Crew! Coming to you live from the road. I met so many of you at VidCon, and it was amazing. I hope all of you will keep in touch. That was, hands down, the very best part of this trip—getting to meet all of you IRL. It's so incredible that we were able to connect online and then bond over technology and movies and girl power in person. The other high point of the trip was—of course—being interviewed by Winter Costello. She'll be posting it on her channel, so check it out. I'm still pinching myself.

"But I should also say, since this is a wrap-up, that the trip wasn't all high points. If not for my low points, though—messing up and learning from my mistakes—I might not even have had the chance to meet you all! Even though I love being behind the camera, and sharing and posting what I create with all of you—meeting you all for real was so much better. That's the biggest thing I learned this summer. I'm going to work hard from now on to be present in the moment, and if I remember to snap a pic and post, so much the better. If I don't, no big deal. So that's been my #summeradventure! Can't wait to see what all of you post about yours. Until next time: Z's Crew, OUT!"

"That sounded like a great post," Mom told me.

"Thanks! I hope so." I settled into my seat and watched out the window as the landscape flew by. Just then, we passed a sign that said WAVE ORGAN–SAN FRANCISCO MARINA: 3.2 MILES.

"'Wave Organ,'" I read aloud. "What's that?"

"Oh, I've always wanted to check that out," Mom

exclaimed. "I've read about it—it's an acoustic sculpture. The water and waves interact with the pipes to produce all sorts of sounds."

"That sounds really cool." I looked over at her. "And it's only three miles away . . ."

"Let's do it!" Mom said as she maneuvered the RV into the right-hand lane.

"Bring it on!" I agreed. "Let our road trip vacation begin!"

I grinned, excited to see something as unusual as the wave organ. I couldn't even imagine what it would be like. I knew, in that moment, that this was the best kind of summer adventure.

No planning—maybe even no filming. Just soaking it all in.

About the *Author*

J. J. Howard was born in a blizzard, but it did *not* lead to a love of snow, so after college she left Pennsylvania for sunny Florida. This plan backfired somewhat because she's now convinced that sixty-five degrees is freezing. By day, J. J. teaches high school English, and at night and on the weekends she writes young adult and middle grade books about characters who enjoy snacks and snarky comments. She's always up for a road trip, as long as she stops for lunch. Her books include *That Time I Joined the Circus* and *Sit, Stay, Love*. Visit her at www.jjhowardbooks.com

Ready
to join

's

Crew?

Visit
americangirl.com to check out Z's vlog!

Meet the 2017 Girl of the Year, Gabriela McBride!
She's a true talent who gets creative for a cause.
Can Gabby use the power of her poetry to save her
beloved community arts center from shutting down?

Turn the page to read a preview of Gabriela's first book!

Like a Roller Coaster

Chapter 1

Toe-heel-toe-heel-toe-heel-STOMP.
Toe-heel-toe-heel-toe-heel-STOMP.

Each move burst into my head like a shout. All around me the air was filled with the sounds of tap shoes scraping and stomping, Mama calling out the next step as she snapped in time to the rhythm of the music. Above me, the sun poured through Liberty's stained-glass windows, leaving little pools of colored light on the floor at my feet.

Riff-heel-ball change-riff-heel-stomp.
Riff-heel-ball change-riff-heel-tuuuuuuurrn.

I stood on my right leg and whirled around, careful to find my spot so I wouldn't get dizzy. My spot was always the same in dance studio number seven: The hollowed-out square cut into the wall right between the two big mirrors.

Gabriela

A phone niche, Mama called it, from the time when phones were so big people had to literally carve out space for them.

Toe-heel-toe-heel-toe-heel-chug.

Toe-heel-scuff-heel-tip-heel-SLAM!

My feet flew over the dance studio's worn wooden floor, from one puddle of light to another, and soon my heart was pounding out a rhythm in time with the beat, like the music and I had become one. I couldn't help it. I closed my eyes. I knew what Mama would say if she caught me: "Gabriela McBride, you know how unsafe that is? And you can lose your place that way!"

I did know that, but I knew Liberty better. Knew every spot on its dance floors, scuffed white from years of dancers like me stomping, turning, and tapping. And I knew that when I opened my eyes, a few beats from now, I'd see Liberty's painted-over brick walls, exposed heating pipes, and its tin-tiled ceiling. And I'd have no trouble finding my place.

"And . . . finish," Mama said as she turned the volume down on the old sound system we used during tap rehearsal. The music faded and then disappeared. I opened my eyes just as Mama began to clap.

"If I didn't know any better," said Mama, "I would think I was in the presence of Savion Glover's dancers."

Like a Roller Coaster

Mama beamed at each member of the Liberty Junior Dance Company in turn. When her eyes met mine, she winked. I winked back.

Mama, or Miss Tina as all the other students called her, was the founder and executive director of Liberty, also known as Liberty Arts Center, a community center she'd started seventeen years ago. Not only was Mama the "Big Kahuna" (that's what Daddy called her), she was also the director of dance programs, which suited her just fine. Mama, with her strong, powerful legs and fluid movements, always said dancing came naturally to her, like breathing. And then she'd say, "It's like that for you, too, Gabby."

It was true. Dancing came to me as easily as coding came to my best friend, Teagan, or the way words came to my cousin, Red. Or the way words seemed to come to almost everyone else, except me.

I glanced up at the clock as Mama instructed us to take a seat on the floor. My heart was still racing, and as the clock crept closer to six, my pulse sped up. I had somewhere important to be.

"Excellent work today, ladies! You're almost ready for our Rhythm and Views show next month."

Five fifty-five. I stared at Mama, willing her eyes to meet mine. When at last she looked over at me, I looked at the clock and back at her. She nodded. She hadn't forgotten she'd given me permission to skip ballet rehearsal and go to the poetry group meeting instead. I half listened as Mama rattled off dates, expectations, and information about costumes.

"Remember how much Rhythm and Views means to Liberty and to the wider community," Mama said. "Sixteen years this show has gone on, and people always come up to me and say—"

I finished Mama's sentence in my head: *that they look forward to this day all year.* The Liberty community loved the show because we got to celebrate all the hard work we'd done in the last year. Art students got to exhibit their work in the lobby and guests could even purchase the artwork, just like at a real art gallery. The dance companies performed the pieces we'd been perfecting all year. An empanada takeout joint from across the street catered the snack bar, and everyone's friends and family came out for the show. It was like a block party, cookout, and concert all rolled into one, and it was my favorite day, too.

Mama finished her speech and then clapped loudly again, her way of signaling that it was time to go.

I jumped to my feet, ran over to where I'd left my bag, and tore off my tap shoes. In four seconds flat, I was bolting toward the door in my sneakers, pausing just long enough to wave to Mama. She smiled and shook her head. I guess she was as surprised as I still sometimes was that I was in a hurry to get to a place where I'd have to stand up and talk in front of other people.

See, talking wasn't like dancing for me. When I danced tap or hip-hop, I could speak with my feet. My hands. My whole body, if I wanted to. I could make one move quiet as a whisper, the next loud as a shout. But sometimes, when I opened my mouth, it was like my words started to second-guess themselves. Like they weren't sure if they wanted to come out and when they finally did, I started stuttering like crazy.

But not all the time.

Like when I was racing to the dance studio where the poetry group met, I ran straight into Amelia Sanchez, my ballet instructor. "Whoa, Gabby, slow down," she said, laughing. "I spoke to your mom. You're going to make up tonight's missed rehearsal, right?"

"I definitely am," I said, without a single stutter.

I kept on going. And when I ran into good old Stan, the friendliest janitor ever, he said, "Where are you hurrying off to, Gabby?" and I replied, "Poetry club meeting. See you later!" without missing a beat.

Gabriela

Mrs. Baxter, my speech therapist at school, told me that people who stutter don't do it as much in places they feel comfortable. That's why my speech was hardly ever bumpy when I was in our little white-and-blue house on Tompkins Street with Mama and Daddy or at Liberty, because both places were home to me, both places filled with family. Like Amelia, who I'd known since she was nineteen and I was six. She taught me how to spot on my turns by challenging me to a staring contest. "Every time you turn, I want us eye-to-eye." Even now, four years later, if Amelia thought I wasn't spotting she'd gently say, "Staring contest, Gabby," to remind me. Stan was like family, too. I'd known him my whole life—he'd been the janitor at Liberty ever since Mama opened it.

"Hold on there now," Stan called out, and I stopped in my tracks. "Poetry's been moved to the auditorium, hasn't it?"

Shoot! How had I forgotten? I took off in the other direction, calling, "Thanks, Stan," over my shoulder as I went.

By the time I made it to the auditorium, the whole group was already up onstage. For the second time, I stopped in my tracks. I'd danced on that very same stage plenty of times, but today was the very first time I'd have to *speak* on it. I gulped.

Like a Roller Coaster

"Gabby, over here!"

Teagan called to me with a frantic wave of her hand. The poetry group had made a circle onstage in front of the heavy red curtain, and Teagan had saved me a seat right beside her.

"I've got everything ready to go," she whispered to me, reaching up to adjust her beanie over her strawberry-blonde hair. There were two things Teagan was almost never without: her coding notebook (she'd named it Cody) and her turquoise beanie.

"Got what ready to go?" I asked.

"The you-know-what that we've been working on?" Teagan wriggled her eyebrows. "You *know*, the *surprise*?"

"Oh, right!" I wiped my sweaty hands on my leggings.

"Are you okay, Gabby?"

"Y-Yes," I stammered. But Teagan knew me better than almost anyone.

"You're nervous about saying your poem in front of Bria and Alejandro, right?" Teagan sat up on her knees and faced me. She was in full-on Teagan Problem-Solving Mode. "Just relax and remember to think about each word before you say it. Give it time to form in your mind. Don't rush. Okay?"

I nodded again. "Okay."

Gabriela

Just then, my cousin Red emerged from behind the curtain, rubbing his hands together and smiling big enough to show off the right front tooth he'd chipped last summer when he hit a curb and flew over the handlebars of his bike. "All right, poets," he said. "Tonight we say bye-bye to that old dance studio and hello to the stage. We're big-time now, ready for crowds skyscraper-high touching clouds."

Red had been staying with my family for the past four months, ever since his mom, Mama's sister and a military doctor, had gotten called back to active duty. At first, I didn't like Red being around too much—for the first few weeks after he arrived, I called him the Interloper until Mama and Daddy told me to stop. But it wasn't my fault Red was *always* in the upstairs bathroom *exactly* when I needed to use it. Plus, he was loud, like two-trains-crashing-into-each-other loud, and he never missed a chance to remind me that he was going into seventh grade and I was only going into sixth.

But, I had to admit Red had a way with words. He could spin a line of poetry like I could pas de bourrée. He lived and breathed poetry, and wanted to bring it to Liberty in the form of a club—nothing too formal. Mama was 100 percent behind the idea and, because I was supposed to be showing Red he was welcome and *not* an interloper, Mama said,

Like a Roller Coaster

"Gabby, you should join, too." She'd made it sound like a suggestion, but it was really an order.

I hadn't wanted to join at first—spoken words are your enemy when you stutter—but words just seemed to flow whenever the poetry group got together. Even mine—most of the time.

"So, the Rhythm and Views show is our first chance to show everyone what we've got," Red was saying.

I imagined Teagan's grandfather, who was the visual arts instructor and the unofficial program director, preparing his art students, too. Everyone—dancers, artists, and this year, poets, too—was a part of Rhythm and Views, and everyone needed to be ready.

"And we need to show them that we've got mad talent," Red was saying. "Which is why everything's got to be perfect. Our poems, the order, everything. Alejandro, can you handle the spotlight for me?"

"On it," Alejandro replied. He was tall and pencil-skinny with thick black hair that came to the middle of his back. Red sometimes liked to joke that Alejandro's hair weighed more than he did. As Alejandro rose and climbed up to the lighting booth, Red pulled a list from the front pocket of his shorts. On it was a list of names. The order of performances. I was first.

Gabriela

First!

"Ready, Gabby?" Red asked. "You can do it. You're big-time now."

"Ready for crowds," a girl named Bria chimed in.

"Skyscraper-high," shouted Alejandro, coming out from the booth at the back of the theater.

"T-Touching clouds," I finished quietly.

"Yes!" Red cried, clapping loudly. Soon everyone else joined in.

As I got to my feet, the applause died down.

"Take center stage, Gabby," Red said, pointing.

I moved to the middle of the circle and looked out at the sea of chairs. The spotlight shined directly on me. *Big-time now, ready for crowds.*

"Sssssspeaking ough-ought to be—" I began, and then I stopped. My face grew hot. I hated stuttering in front of my friends. Maybe I could tell Red to come back to me at the end.

"You were doing great, Gabby," Alejandro called out.

"Keep going," said Red.

"Slow down and think about each word," Teagan put in.

Mama and Daddy were always telling me that while it was good to work with Mrs. Baxter, I shouldn't let my bumpy speech stop me from talking. "We love you no matter how many sounds you make," they'd say. "Say what you have to say! We're always listening."

"Okay." Another deep breath. Then I started over.

"Speaking ought to be, ought to be like . . . like
      breathing
Words always there, no need for . . . reaching
Like cracking a jjjjjjoke is for a joker
But for me it's like a roller coaster . . . coaster"

I paused. I knew this poem and even bigger than that, I knew these people. Red. Teagan. Alejandro. Bria. I knew this space, too, Liberty's auditorium. I knew there were 480 seats, but only 476 worked. I knew seat 3L was the best in the house, that one of the angels carved into the balcony was cross-eyed, and that there was a corner where every word you said echoed throughout the auditorium, even if you whispered. *You're home, Gabby,* I told myself, and picked up my poem where I left off.

"Up, up, up and then racing . . . racing to the
      g-ground

Gabriela

Words flying by me that I can't pin down

Words soar past me, whip my face like . . . like air
In my mind, in my heart, everywhere
I . . . I ch-chase those wwwwords down
But when I try to speak, I don't make a sound

Up, up, up and then racing to the ground
Words flying by me that I can't pin down

Sometimes my words get caught
Come grinding to a halt
I slip, I fall, I stutter
But it's not my fault

Up, up, up and then racing to the ground
Words flying by me that I can't pin down."

The applause was instantaneous. So was my smile. I'd made it through my whole poem, and by the end I wasn't stuttering at all! I took a deep, exaggerated bow. And then another, and then curtsied until the rest of the poetry group was either laughing or calling out, "Brava, brava!" or "Encore, encore!"

Like a Roller Coaster

Red, still beaming, held up his hand for silence. "No time for encores, but awesome job, Gabby." He walked over and gave me a high five. "Bria, you're up."

Bria, a tall, round-faced girl with a big, bushy ponytail, took center stage as I slid back into my place next to Teagan. Bria, like Alejandro and Red, was going into seventh grade and when Red had told her about the poetry group, she'd joined immediately.

"Nice job," Teagan mouthed. Then she reached into the pocket of her jeans and pulled out a flash drive. "Ready for later?" she whispered.

I nodded. I felt ready for anything.

The rest of the performances flew by, and I still couldn't believe how far we'd all come since Red had first started the poetry club. And even more than that, I couldn't wait for the show. Poetry, dancing, and—

"Gabby and I have a surprise," Teagan announced, just as Alejandro, the final poet, took his seat. "We've been working on something for the show, a little something visual to go with our poetry. Wait right here."

Teagan jumped to her feet, pulling me with her. We darted around the curtain and backstage, where there was a laptop sitting on top of a podium. Wires snaked down the side of the podium like vines. To anyone else all of those wires would have been intimidating. But not to Teagan. In one smooth motion, she plugged the projector adapter into the laptop, inserted her flash drive, and said, "Can you get the main power switch for the podium and projector?" She pointed at a black box hanging on the wall behind us. It looked like a very large, very expensive version of the circuit breaker in our garage, only, I realized after pulling the box open, much more complicated. Inside were three rows of buttons and switches, all glowing a faint shade of neon green.

"Um, Teagan?"

"On it," Teagan replied, and hurried over. She pointed at a big silver button on top of all the others. "This one turns on the main power for all the stage equipment. It's kind of cool how it all works. You see, this main box controls—"

"Teagan," I cut in. Sometimes, when Teagan started talking tech, she couldn't stop.

"Sorry!" Teagan said, laughing. "Ready?"

I nodded. We reached for the button, both of our fingers pushing it at the same time.

And everything went black.

Parents, request a FREE catalogue at
americangirl.com/catalogue

Sign up at **americangirl.com/email**
to receive the latest news and exclusive offers